to kiss a thief...

A new fear fluttered in Cristy's breast.

But it wasn't dread.

It was anticipation.

Her gaze fell to Brochan's mouth, and she couldn't help but wonder what it would be like to press her lips to his, to melt into his welcoming arms, to feel perfectly safe and protected.

She let out the breath she'd been holding. It came out on a tremble.

She was going to do it. She couldn't help herself. She was going to kiss him.

Brochan couldn't believe he was going to kiss her. Every instinct told him not to. No good would come of it. He could think of at least a dozen good reasons not to do such a reckless thing. And he would list them all...right after he finished the kiss.

Cover design by Richard Campbell
Formatting by Author E.M.S.

Glynnis Campbell – Publisher
P.O. Box 341144
Arleta, California 91331
ISBN-10: 163480-030-3
ISBN-13: 978-1-63480-030-3
Contact: glynnis@glynnis.net

Published in the United States of America.

The Reiver

The Prequel Novella to Medieval Outlaws

OTHER BOOKS BY GLYNNIS CAMPBELL

THE WARRIOR MAIDS OF RIVENLOCH
The Shipwreck (novella)
Lady Danger
Captive Heart
Knight's Prize

THE KNIGHTS OF DE WARE
The Handfasting (novella)
My Champion
My Warrior
My Hero

MEDIEVAL OUTLAWS
The Reiver (novella)
Danger's Kiss
Passion's Exile
Desire's Ransom

THE SCOTTISH LASSES
The Outcast (novella)
MacFarland's Lass
MacAdam's Lass
MacKenzie's Lass

THE CALIFORNIA LEGENDS
Native Gold
Native Wolf
Native Hawk

ACKNOWLEDGMENTS

My sincerest thanks to

my sisters in The Summer Star,
Tanya Anne Crosby and Laurin Wittig,
for inspiring the legend;
my niece Rayna Barden
for sharing her knowledge of livestock;
my husband Richard Campbell,
for taking me on the best adventures;
my amazing Readers Clan,
for their love and support;
and Michelle Rodriguez and Chris Pratt
for their inspiration

For Barb Batlan-Massabrook
and Deborah Stewart,
two of the toughest "Scottish" lasses I know

CHAPTER 1

Summer 1211
Dumfries, Scotland

Brighde felt the star coming long before anyone spied it in the night sky.

She could feel it in the way she felt the brush of a spider's web or the faint caress of a breeze, the distant drone of honeybees or the delicate kiss of morning mist.

Every seventy-five years it came. Like a spark struck from a smith's anvil, it streaked across the black night. For several days it hung in the heavens, sweeping close to the earth, lighting up heath and braes.

Some feared it would drop from the sky and set the world ablaze.

Brighde knew better. The star's course never strayed.

But it did possess a singular magic—the power of

transformation. And that power was dangerous, for it could be used for either good or evil.

Some claimed the star brought bad luck. They blamed it for fire and flood, famine and misfortune.

But those who believed in the goodness of the star were granted rebirth, renewal, redemption—a chance to begin again.

Brighde smiled as she tossed her shimmering golden locks over her shoulder and pulled the tap, filling her patron's wooden flagon with ale.

Two lost souls whose fates would be changed by the star were about to cross Brighde's path. She could feel it in her bones. One, the lass, was coming later this eve. The other was already on his way.

She turned toward the gap-toothed old soldier who'd plunked his coin down for a pint and gave him a brilliant smile.

"There ye go, lad," she sang.

If he gave her a quizzical look for calling a man who appeared to be twice her age "lad," she didn't pay much heed. Her attention was centered, not on the soldier, but on the door. In another moment, *he* would arrive.

Brochan Macintosh didn't really know why he was stopping at the inn. After all, he needed to get home to his young sons. He'd been gone for hours. And he hated to leave Colin and Cambel in the hands of his already overworked housekeeper.

For the last several weeks, he'd inhabited the tower

house on the holding he'd inherited from his uncle, the former Laird of Macintosh. But the old laird must have grown daft or penniless over the last few years, for when Brochan arrived, the keep was deserted and half in ruins.

Brochan was doing most of the repairs himself—fixing leaks in the roof, replacing cracked timbers, rebuilding rotted stairs—while his two faithful servants swept out the moldy rushes, chased mice from the buttery, kept the household fed, and watched over his sons.

To have five of his cattle go missing in the last week only added to Brochan's long list of problems to solve. He'd searched for hours today for the lost cows, scouring acres of the thick woods that made up the border of his property, to no avail.

Perhaps that was why he felt he deserved to stop for an ale at the roadside inn before he trudged home.

Throwing back the hood of his gray tartan brat, he ducked under the thatched roof and pushed open the heavy door. The inn was cheery inside, lit by tallow candles and a lively peat fire. He nodded a greeting to the old man seated by the hearth, the only patron in the inn at this hour. Then he untied the wooden cup from his belt and approached the bar.

When he set down his cup, he almost knocked it over, so rattled was he by the tavern wench beaming at him from the other side. She was as bright as an angel and as beautiful as a goddess. Her golden tresses spilled over her perfect bosom like honey. Her skin glowed as if lit from within. Her smile was as open, pure, and enchanting as a child's.

But that wasn't what made his cup stutter on the bar. Her eyes, like rare crystal, caught the light and reflected it back in mutable shades of green and blue.

"Good day," she said. "I'm Brighde, at your service. What will ye have?"

Her voice was as lovely as her appearance. And yet he couldn't help but compare her to that other beauty, the one who'd been taken away from him. No woman would ever measure up to his lovely wife, the mother of his sons. She'd been dead for five years. But his heart still ached when he thought about her sweet freckled face and her sky-blue eyes.

"Ale, please," he said quietly.

Brighde took his cup and started filling it from the tap. "What are ye up to this fine summer's day?"

"Not much," he said.

"Indeed?" Her expression was amused, skeptical.

He reconsidered. Maybe the tavern wench had information about his lost cows. "Actually, I'm searchin' for my cattle. Some o' them have gone missin'. Ye haven't heard anythin' about any coos runnin' loose, have ye?"

Brighde handed him his full cup. "Coos," she mused.

He pulled a coin from his pouch for the ale and set it on the bar, then tossed back a healthy swig.

When Brighde picked up the coin, her eyes were twinkling. "'Tis a band o' reivers after your coos," she told him.

"What?"

"Reivers have stolen your cattle."

He frowned. "Reivers? What reivers?"

"Och, that I can't tell ye."

"Then how do ye know 'tis reivers and not—"

"They're comin' again tonight."

"What?"

"The reivers. They're comin' again. Tonight."

Brochan lowered his brows. The lass seemed very sure of that. What wasn't she telling him? "Look, lass, if ye know somethin'..."

"Aye. I know somethin'." Her eyes had taken on an unsettling silvery shade now, as if she were gazing into another world. "Watch for the reivers to return tonight. Ye'll get your coos back...and more."

More? What the devil did that mean?

Before he could ask her, she captured his eyes with her own, burning into them with blue-green fire, and the words suddenly fled from his mind. She murmured tenderly, "And ye'll no longer be lonely."

He gulped. Lonely? What made her think he was lonely? Brochan wasn't lonely. He was rarely ever alone. He had his two sons. His two servants. And, until recently, a whole herd of cows. The woman must be mistaken.

Tearing his gaze away, he scoffed, "Lonely? I'm not lonely."

Yet something about the way she'd spoken snagged at his heart. Something about his reply was empty and false. And something about the way she was gazing at him now—compassion softening her eyes to a gentle gray—made him believe she was peeking between his words of denial, peering at the truth. A truth he refused to admit, even to himself.

Her eyes lost all their frost then, darkening to a friendly blue, and she smiled. "Ye know, your stars are about to change, lad."

He lifted a dubious brow. Had the young miss just called him a lad? "My stars."

"Aye. But 'tis up to ye whether ye lay claim to that fate," she intoned, "or let it pass ye by."

He took another cautious sip at his ale. "I see." He didn't see, not at all. Indeed, he was beginning to wonder if Brighde's great beauty was compensation for a lack of wits.

"The star has chosen ye," she said.

"The star," he repeated.

The poor lass *was* mad. All stars did was light up the night sky.

He sighed. He knew he shouldn't have wandered into the inn.

He finished his ale in a gulp and tied the empty cup back onto his belt. But before he could turn away, Brighde seized his hands in hers.

It startled him, especially when a warm vibration began to flow up his arms. Yet, even more startling, he felt no panic, no desire to pull away.

"Remember," she whispered, gazing into his eyes with blue-green intensity. "Your destiny is in your hands."

When she released him, he felt shaken to his core. But he wasn't about to let her know it. Instead, he thanked her for the ale and turned to go. Faith, he had to get back home, back to people who believed destiny was determined, not by stars, but by hard work.

Still, as he plodded down the road toward the tower house, he wondered if Brighde's comment about reivers had merit. It hadn't occurred to him that his cows might have been intentionally stolen. But considering the chilly welcome Brochan had received from the local folk on moving into the tower, it was entirely possible that a couple of the hostile neighbor lads had thieved his cattle.

He decided there was naught to be lost by keeping a watchful eye on his herd tonight.

Cristy Moffat picked up her inconvenient skirts, cursing her throbbing ankle and struggling to keep up with her cousins. Her lungs were burning. But she didn't want to get left behind.

The lads were always leaving her behind. It was bad enough that, even at eighteen, she was a wee lass and couldn't match their long stride. But ever since she'd twisted her ankle at supper, every step sent a twinge up her leg.

It had been a stupid accident, entirely her fault. Serving her uncle pottage, she'd tripped over her cousin's stray foot and slopped the soup into her uncle's lap.

She supposed she deserved the clout he'd given her for her clumsiness. And it wasn't the first time he'd called her a worthless lass. At least the black eye and the insult didn't hurt like her ankle did.

Of course, she wasn't about to let her cousins know she was in pain. If she did, they'd tell her she had to stay home. And more than anything, she wanted to come along.

Each of the five lads had taken a turn, creeping out at night to reive a cow from their new neighbor, Macintosh. Tonight was her turn. And she didn't intend to miss her chance.

Her uncle didn't much care for Macintosh, the new owner of the tower house and land adjoining his. Her uncle didn't like strangers, especially those with more cattle than he had. So he'd crowed with glee over his sons' stealth and trickery, happy to add another cow to his own herd at Macintosh's expense.

Cristy was determined to show her cousins that she could reive cattle as well as any lad. And she meant to prove to her uncle that he was wrong, that she wasn't entirely worthless.

"Come on, runt!" Fergus yelled back at her as they headed toward the starlit inn. "We haven't got all night."

She heard Doug mutter, "I told ye this was a mistake."

"Shite, Cristy!" Morris jeered. "Ye won't even catch a calf at that speed."

Hamish grumbled, "She'll probably go for the bull and break her neck."

"I'm comin'," she insisted, hobbling forward. "I'm just...I'm savin' it for tonight."

Archibald, the oldest, shook his head. "We shouldn't have brought her. I've got a bad feelin' about this."

Cristy raised a determined chin as they gathered outside the inn. "I can do it. I'll show ye."

"Sure ye will," Morris sneered.

"I *will*," Cristy insisted.

"If ye don't get a coo," Hamish threatened, "that's it.

No more taggin' along like ye're one of us."

His words crushed her. But she'd learned to hide that kind of pain long ago. The pain of not belonging.

He was right. She wasn't one of them. But after the death of her parents seven years ago, her uncle and her cousins were all she had. If she lost them...

She gulped back her fear.

She couldn't afford to fail. So she forced a cocky smile to her lips. With a confidence she didn't feel, she said, "I'll do it. Ye just watch me."

Rolling his eyes, Fergus pushed open the door of the inn, and they all crowded inside.

Last to enter, Cristy closed the door behind her and tossed back the hood of her brown arisaid, dragging out her long black braid. A merry fire crackled on the hearth. A handful of patrons sat at tables, laughing and drinking foamy cups of ale. Her cousins were quick to claim the largest table against the wall.

Before she could slide onto the bench beside Archibald, Hamish flipped a silver coin onto the table in front of her. "Be a good lass, and fetch us all ales."

They unbuckled the wooden cups from their belts and set them on the table in front of her.

Cristy snapped up the coin, took the five cups by their handles, and headed across the room to the bar, where the tavern wench was pulling ale.

She set the coin and the cups on the bar, adding her own.

When the woman turned toward her, Cristy gave a little gasp. She was the most beautiful lady Cristy had ever seen. Her skin glowed like a candle, and the tresses framing her face shone like spun gold. Her lips curved up as if she kept some delicious secret, and her eyes sparkled like the surface of a stream, in varying shades of blue, green, and silver. It was hard to say how old she was. She looked both as fresh as a newborn babe and as worldly as an ancient sage.

Obviously, Cristy's cousins hadn't seen the breathtaking wench. If they had, they'd have fallen all over themselves for the privilege of speaking to her.

"Good even," the woman said. Even her voice was beautiful, like the soft, melodic tones of a harp. "I'm Brighde, at your service. What will ye—" She broke off abruptly. Black lightning flashed in her gaze, then vanished as quickly as it had struck. She was staring at Cristy's bruise. "Where did ye get that?"

Cristy raised her fingers to her cheek. She'd all but forgotten about her injury. She supposed she should have kept her face hidden so as not to trouble anyone.

"'Tis naught," she said with a shrug. "Just an acci—"

But Brighde suddenly seized her wrist and pulled her forward. "Let me see."

Cristy scowled. How dare the woman grab her? And why was she making such a great fuss? It was only a black eye, after all.

She tried to pull away, but Brighde was having none of it. The woman lifted Cristy's chin to take a closer look. Then her eyes softened to the color of fog.

Cristy wished she wouldn't look at her like that, with kindness and pity. It made her uncomfortable. She squirmed out of Brighde's grasp, avoiding the woman's eyes. "Six ales, please."

With a nod, Brighde set out a tray and began to fill the cups from the tap. As she did, she dispensed an unwelcome bit of advice along with the ale. "Ye shouldn't let them treat ye like that, orderin' ye about like a servant."

Cristy blinked. What concern was it of a tavern wench's how her cousins treated her? Unsure what to say, she smirked and shrugged. "They're kin."

"Did one o' them give ye that mark?" she asked, nodding at Cristy's eye.

"Nay," Cristy said defensively.

Brighde began filling the second cup. "But 'twas a man. A man with a hot temper, aye?"

Cristy frowned. She owed the woman no explanation. But somehow the words came tumbling out before she could stop them. "'Twas only my uncle. I tripped and spilled pottage on him."

Brighde placed the full cup on the tray, arching her perfect brows. "He clouted you—for an accident?"

"I suppose so." It did sound wrong when she said it like that. But Brighde didn't know the situation. And Cristy didn't feel like explaining that she'd always been a clumsy fool.

Brighde was silent a long while as she filled three more cups. "So what are ye and your lads up to this even?"

"Cristy!" Morris yelled. "What's takin' ye so bloody long?"

"Comin'!" she shouted back. Then, because she was

impatient with Brighde—who seemed to be taking her time and sticking her nose where it didn't belong—Cristy snapped, "I don't think 'tis any o' your bloody concern what I'm doin' this even."

Instead of the shocked gasp Cristy expected, Brighde glanced up at her with a curious smile on her lips. "Well, they haven't crushed *all* your spirit yet, have they?"

Cristy furrowed her brows. What was that supposed to mean?

"Ye know, lass, it doesn't have to be like this," Brighde said, placing the last cup before her.

"Like what?"

She leaned forward to whisper, "Tryin' so hard to belong."

A queer tingling started at the back of Cristy's neck. Brighde's glittering eyes seemed to change color, shifting from green to blue and back again. Cristy felt as if the woman was reaching inside her mind, inside her soul, reading her thoughts and heart.

"Change is on the horizon," Brighde told her, penetrating deep into her eyes. "Your stars are about to transform. Fate hangs in the balance. *Your* fate."

Cristy had no idea what the woman was talking about, but something about Brighde's words and the way she was staring made her shiver.

Brighde reached out then and seized Cristy's hand, placing it between both of hers. Cristy gasped. The woman's palms were charged with some mysterious current, like the crackle of static in the north wind that preceded a shock. But Cristy couldn't pull away.

She knew she should be afraid. She could feel Brighde's strength, her will, her force. And yet, gazing into the woman's exquisite and kindly face, she felt no fear.

"The star has chosen ye," Brighde softly intoned. "The rest is in your hands. 'Tis up to ye whether ye seize the day..." As if making her point, she released Cristy's hand, "Or let it escape through your fingers."

Cristy glanced at her hand, half expecting it to be transformed into something else.

With a gentle smile, Brighde placed the mugs full of ale on the tray and handed it to her. "Your future beckons," she murmured. "Follow it, and ye may change your fate."

"Cristy!" shouted Hamish. "Move your arse!"

She winced. "Comin'!"

She turned to thank Brighde for the ales. But the woman had already moved away and was attending to a pair of gape-jawed drunks.

Cristy picked her cautious way to the table. She didn't want to trip over her own feet again.

"What took ye so bloody long?" Archibald demanded, passing out the ales. He added in a mutter, "'Twill be midnight by the time we get to Macintosh's."

He didn't expect an answer, and she didn't give him one. But as the lads gulped their ale, elbowed each other, and made ribald remarks about the toothsome tavern wench they'd finally noticed behind the bar, Cristy was lost in her thoughts.

Even after they left the inn for the long walk to the

Macintosh holding, she couldn't get the curious woman's words out of her head.

What had Brighde meant?

What future was she talking about?

Was she some kind of seer?

Or was she only mad?

They continued along the road by the long-lasting light of summer until they reached the narrow burn that divided the two properties—her uncle's and Macintosh's. From there, they'd leave the main road so as not to be spotted. It was still a long hike over heather-covered braes and through soggy bogs to reach the place near the tower house where the cattle bedded down for the night.

But if what Brighde had said was true—if Cristy's fate would change tonight—she didn't intend to let anything, even her twisted ankle, prevent her from making the journey.

CHAPTER 2

"**W**here are ye goin', Da?" wee Colin asked as Brochan buckled on his sword over his white leine and black trews. The lad's brows were furrowed, and his five-year-old eyes looked fretful.

Brochan hunkered down and clasped the lad's wee shoulder.

"Nowhere. Just out to the fields. Now I'm countin' on ye lads to keep watch while I'm gone." He reached over to squeeze Cambel's shoulder as well. Then he glanced up and gave his man, Rauf, a wink.

Cambel didn't look convinced. He glanced at Brochan's sword. "How long will ye be gone, Da?"

"Och, not long at all."

Brochan exchanged a meaningful look with Rauf. He *hoped* he wouldn't be long. If they returned, he was determined to catch the damned reivers tonight.

He was convinced now the tavern wench was right. It

was reivers who'd taken his cows. The nasty thieves had already stolen five of them in as many days. Tonight he would stand watch over the herd. If the villains tried to strike again, he'd be ready for them.

"Why can't I come, Da?" Colin asked, his green eyes serious. "I'll be careful around the coos."

"Me too," Cambel chimed in. "And I'm not afraid o' the dark."

Brochan smiled and ruffled the twins' unruly auburn hair that looked so like their mother's. "Ye're two brave lads, that's for sure. But I need ye here. After all, ye can't expect Rauf to watch o'er the keep all by himself."

"That's right," Rauf said, lowering his gray brows to give them a stern frown. "'Tis up to us to guard the house."

Rauf's wife, Mabel, called out from where she was tending the fire. "I'm countin' on ye braw lads to keep me safe."

Brochan grinned at that. Keep her safe indeed. Mabel was as big as a tree, as strong as an ox, and as unyielding as iron. If required, she could probably roust the entire English army from the tower house.

In fact, once she heard about Brochan's intentions to waylay the reivers, Mabel had offered to go after the good-for-naught knaves herself. But Brochan wasn't about to let her tangle with outlaws. She was too valuable as a cook and a nursemaid to his sons to be risking her life over such nonsense.

Brochan was grateful Rauf and Mabel had come with him to this new holding. The loyal servants had been

with him since the lads were born. He didn't know what he'd do without them.

This battle with the reivers, however, was Brochan's. He was fairly sure that reiving his cattle was his unfriendly neighbors' attempt to chase him off.

It wouldn't work. He was determined to stay. He'd come too far and surrendered too much to go back now. He wouldn't let a few hostile neighbors frighten him away, especially since he had no intention of returning to the place where he'd met and married his beloved wife. There were too many painful reminders of her there.

It was best he make a fresh start. On this sizeable plot of land with its grassy, rolling braes and its thick forests, its lovely winding burn and its crumbling-but-reparable tower house, he could raise his sons in peace—far away from their mother's kin, who, though they never spoke of it aloud, silently blamed the twins for her death.

Brochan gave Cambel and Colin a kiss on the brow. How anyone could blame his two precious sons for anything so tragic, he didn't know.

"Ye do what Rauf tells ye now," he reminded them.

The lads nodded. Brochan straightened, adjusting his sword belt. He wore his sword out of habit. He doubted he'd need a weapon. The reivers were likely just a couple of lads up to mischief.

They would quickly learn that Brochan Macintosh was not a man to sit idly by while his cattle were picked off. A stern word from him about the foolishness of stealing from one's neighbor and the return of his cows should set the matter to rights.

The evening air was mild and pleasant. The sky was still not fully dark as he headed down the steep slope of the motte toward the glen where the cows usually spent the night. The dark green pines of the forest were etched in jagged silhouettes against the violet sky. Stars were just emerging, sprinkled like salt across the heavens. Thistles of starlit purple studded the grass like gems.

The crickets stopped chirping as he hiked across the spongy loam. In the well-grazed pasture, he could make out the rough, dark shapes of horned black cows slumbering on the sod.

Angling across the brae, he found a good vantage point where he could hide in a clump of tall heather and view the whole glen. He settled onto his seat on the damp ground, rested his arms on his raised knees, and narrowed his eyes at the herd below.

The crickets gradually resumed their singing. Now and then a cow would stir, raising its shaggy head and lowering it again. Brochan sat as still as stone while the moon slowly moved across the sky.

As always, when he was alone and unoccupied, memories of his wife seeped into his thoughts. Even after five years, he missed her. He hated to admit it was getting harder and harder to remember her face. But the features their sons had inherited from her—her reddish-brown hair, her freckled nose, her stubborn chin—haunted him. It was a blessing the lads had been born with green eyes like Brochan's, for he didn't think he could endure seeing his wife's merry sky-blue eyes every day.

He still wasn't past blaming himself for her death. Recalling her pale and shivering body as she delivered their second twin with her last breath, he felt crushing guilt, even though he'd done everything he could to save her life. Everything except stay away from her bed in the first place.

He swallowed the lump in his throat. It was too late for regrets now. She was gone, and he'd never find another like her. He had to do the best he could for their sons on his own.

As he surveyed the great glen that was now part of his holding, his eye caught on a curious star he hadn't seen before above the distant brae. It was lower than the others. And though it appeared motionless in the sky, a long stream of light trailed after it like a tail.

A comet, he realized in wonder. He hadn't seen a comet since he was a lad. He'd never seen one so vivid nor so close to the earth. Now he wished he *had* brought Colin and Cambel out to the field with him.

He narrowed his eyes. If it was like the comet he'd seen before, it would appear every night for several days as it slowly crossed the heavens. He'd be sure to show it to his sons tomorrow night then, just as his father had done for him all those years ago.

Most people believed that comets were a portent of things to come. Some thought they brought bad luck. Some thought they were harbingers of good fortune.

Brochan figured they were no more than an interesting feature in the night sky that men could only partly understand, like falling stars or eclipses. Still, if the comet wished to bring him good luck, he'd be grateful for the return of his cattle.

His eyes shifted suddenly as they caught movement coming from the edge of the woods. He stiffened. He could make out the shadowy shapes of six cloaked figures stealing out of the forest, not forty yards away.

Brochan moved his hand to the hilt of his sword. Maybe it was good he'd brought it after all. Never had he imagined he'd have to deal with an entire army of reivers.

At the edge of the trees, they all stopped, all but the smallest one. That one continued to slowly advance. The reiver had chosen his target carefully. The lone cow was at a little distance from the rest of the herd, at a good distance from the bull, and she had no calf with her.

In the same way the reiver meant to separate the cow from the herd to make it easier to capture, Brochan could separate the lad from the rest of his companions. If he could steal down the brae without being spotted, he could easily grab the thief and use him as leverage to quell the rest of his fellows.

The reiver clearly knew what he was doing. He took his time, letting the cows adjust to his presence, and headed in a straight line toward his target. Though Brochan couldn't make out the words, he could hear the lad's low, soothing murmurs as he calmed the cattle.

Slowly, Brochan eased up from the ground, creeping forward through the heather, keeping his eyes trained on his prey.

Then a curious thing happened. The reiver stopped abruptly, went silent, and straightened.

Brochan realized the lad was staring at the sky.

He'd seen the star.

Brochan glanced toward the other reivers. They were pointing at the comet and jostling each other, as though arguing over it.

Finally, one of them hissed at the lone reiver in the moonlight, beckoning him.

But the reiver stood frozen in the field, awestruck.

While they were thus distracted, Brochan made his swift way down the rise.

He was no more than twenty yards away when the tallest reiver spotted him. The lad cursed and shoved at his companions, and the lot of them retreated under the trees.

All of them but the reiver in the field, who paid no heed to their calls or Brochan's presence. The lad lingered in the moonlight, transfixed by the comet, as Brochan crept closer and closer.

Cristy stared, struck dumb by the vision in the heavens.

What was that? A star? Or something else?

It wasn't moving. Yet a long, feathery tail stretched out behind it as if it were flying across the night sky.

She'd never seen such a thing.

"Cristy, come on!" Archibald hissed from the trees. "Now, damn ye!"

She ignored him. She didn't care about the cows now. She could catch a cow another night. This was far more intriguing.

Suddenly she remembered what the tavern wench had told her.

Change is on the horizon. The star has chosen ye. Follow it, and ye may change your fate.

She shivered. Was this her star? Had Brighde truly foreseen her future?

In one moment, she was gazing at the star in wonder.

In the next, she was hurtling toward the ground.

When her shoulder hit the sod, her first thought was that the bull had charged and knocked her over.

But when she tried to scramble out of harm's way, a heavy arm held her down—a human arm.

"Archibald," she bit out, for she was sure it was her oldest cousin, "let me up."

"Hold still."

Cristy's eyes went wide. It wasn't her cousin. She didn't recognize the voice.

"Ye'll frighten the coos," he warned.

If it wasn't her cousins, it must be one of Macintosh's men.

Shite! She couldn't be caught. Reiving cattle was a serious crime.

Deciding she'd rather take her chances with the herd of frightened cows than with their vengeful owner, she spat out a curse, then struggled and bucked and kicked and scratched, trying to free herself from the clutches of her captor. But he was very persistent and very strong.

Through the strands of her hair, she glimpsed her cousins hiding under the trees. Why weren't they helping her? She grimaced as the arm around her waist tightened.

And then she heard the cattle. All the noise was disturbing them.

Good, she thought. Maybe the restless cows would distract the beast attacking her long enough for her to escape.

She took in a deep breath, ready to yell for all she was worth.

Her cry was cut short by the clap of a huge hand over her mouth.

"Hush!" the man hissed against her ear. "Ye'll get us both killed if that bull charges."

Cristy glanced again toward the trees. Her cousins had vanished.

Her heart sank. If they'd abandoned her, she was as good as dead. So what did she care if the bull killed her?

She renewed her struggles.

In the end, it was no use. Her captor, whoever he was, had a grip like iron and a will to match. He hefted her up like a fleece of wool in one powerful arm, muffling her cries with his sweaty palm, and packed her off across the field toward the tower house.

Her last thought as she caught one final glimpse of the strange star in the sky was that Brighde had only promised her a change of fortune.

She hadn't said it might be a change for the worse.

Brochan realized about halfway through subduing the reiver that the scrappy firebrand he'd caught was a lass. But by then, it was too late to let her go. She was already riling up the cattle. He had to get her away from them.

The cows were by nature fairly calm. Brochan let his sons pet the shaggy beasts, as long as they were with him. Twice a day, the lads milked the two cows that had lost their young in the byre. But some of the cows in the field had young calves they were protecting. And the bull was unpredictable.

Even if Brochan had wanted to let her go, the wee reiver's companions had deserted her. And he wasn't about to let a lass roam the countryside by night all alone. He'd never be able to live with himself if she were attacked by wolves or miscreants.

So, regretting his rough handling of the lass, he proceeded to remove her from the field as efficiently as possible.

Any regret he had was cut short when, halfway up the brae, the minx bit into the soft part of his palm.

With an outcry that was more aggravation than pain, he yanked his hand away.

She took a breath.

No doubt she meant to curse him.

Or cry for help.

Or scream at the top of her lungs.

He couldn't have her doing any of those. So he stuffed a wad of her arisaid into her open mouth before she could make a peep.

But like plugging a wasp's nest, his actions only served to agitate her further. She thrashed and twisted in the prison of his arms. Her anger erupted in frustrated squeals behind the stifling wool.

She was still fighting him and screaming into her arisaid when he climbed the motte and reached the tower house door. But he didn't have a free hand. So, grimacing in anticipation of her curses, he uncovered her mouth long enough to reach for the handle.

She didn't disappoint. As he swung open the door, she spat the wool from her mouth and emitted a string of oaths vile enough to make the devil blush.

Even the stalwart Rauf, who rushed forward to close the door behind them, blinked at the foul curses.

Eager to be rid of his noisy burden, Brochan carried the lass into the hall and set her abruptly on her feet, so abruptly she nearly tripped on the hem of her kirtle.

She tossed her head, and her long black braid slapped him in the face. He had just enough time to see her snarling white teeth—the teeth now imprinted upon his palm—before she did the unthinkable.

While he was disentangling himself from the hissing she-cat, the lass laid her hands upon the hilt of his sword and pulled it from its sheath.

Brochan leaped back just in time to avoid the edge of the blade. It whistled past, missing him by inches.

Before he even had time to curse himself for his carelessness, she stabbed forward. He fell back, grabbing a lit sconce from the wall to use as a weapon.

"Put the sword down," he warned.

She glared at him through damp strands of her dark hair, but still she held the blade aloft in both hands.

"Put it down," he repeated.

When she refused to comply, he lunged forward

with the sconce, forcing her to skitter back.

With a determined growl, she slashed again and again at the space between them. Her swings were reckless and wildly unpredictable.

Defending himself with the sconce, he managed to keep her from doing too much damage.

"Nay, Rauf!" he barked at his man, who was trying to sneak up on the lass. "Stay back!"

He didn't want anyone injured by a stray blade. Besides, if Brochan couldn't handle this minikin of a lass on his own, he didn't deserve to be laird of the tower house.

"Whoreson!" the lass spat. "Satan's spawn!"

Brochan frowned. He wondered if she kissed the lads with that filthy mouth.

She took another swipe at him, and he fended it off with the sconce, extinguishing the candle.

He could have brought the heavy piece down on her head at that point and knocked her out. But he hated to resort to such violence when it wasn't necessary.

Besides, the way the lass was fighting—with all her pluck and every bit of her strength—she couldn't last much longer. He'd just wait for her to tire.

"Ye hedge-born bastard!"

Brochan shook his head and deflected another wayward swing.

As he did, he caught a glimpse of Cambel and Colin, who'd heard the noise and come downstairs. They peered out from the shadows of the stairwell with their wooden swords in hand, ready to do battle.

He grimaced. They'd probably witnessed the whole sordid incident and were hanging on every blasphemous word.

CHAPTER 3

Cristy dared not show it, but she'd never been so scared in her life.

The evening couldn't have gone more wrong.

Her cousins had deserted her.

She'd been captured and spirited away by the enemy.

A fiery star was headed for the earth.

And now she was fighting with a weapon so heavy she could scarcely wield it—against a man who looked as big as an ox.

He was going to kill her. She knew it.

He'd caught her going after his cattle. And now he was going to make her pay.

Her heart was pounding. Her palms were sweating. But she knew she couldn't show an ounce of fear. For if she did, he would surely finish her on the spot.

So she tossed her braid over her shoulder, kicked her skirts out of the way, and attacked again, cursing at him

with courage she didn't possess. "The devil rot ye *and* your coos!"

"Na-a-a-a-y!" A high-pitched war cry announced a young child in a long white leine as he came running out of the shadows toward her, wielding a wee wooden sword.

She hesitated an instant, and a second child followed, looking like a mirror image of the first.

Before she could even blink in astonishment, the man she'd been fighting bellowed, "Nay!"

In one sudden movement, he dropped the sconce and lunged for her, heedless of her sword.

His momentum knocked her backwards so hard, she was sure her head would crack upon the stones. But at the last instant, he turned with her, cushioning her head with one hand and landing mostly on his shoulder.

"Stay back, lads!" he called out to the children.

His warning was unnecessary. The fall had loosened her grip on the sword. It had clattered out of reach on the rushes.

He rolled her quickly on her back, straddling her and pinning her wrists to the floor.

Now she was helpless. And frightened. If she wasn't careful, she'd erupt in full-scale panic, which would give him even more of an upper hand.

But then she peered at the man through the disheveled veil of her hair. The blood had drained from his face. He had a fretful look in his eyes. He looked as if...as if he'd expected her to run those children through with the sword.

Now her fear gave way to outrage and anger.

She frowned and spit a lock of her hair from her mouth. Did he really believe her capable of such violence? She might reive a cow or two, and she would definitely stand up to an ox like him. But she didn't slay innocents in cold blood.

"God's eyes," she muttered, "I wouldn't have harmed them."

He stared down at her with such ferocity that she couldn't look away. "Hurt my sons," he bit out so softly she could scarcely hear it, "and I'll kill ye."

She gulped. A dark fire burned in his emerald eyes, searing her soul. His sons. He must love them fiercely to make such a vow.

Finally, growing apprehensive beneath his intense glare, she mumbled, "What kind o' monster do ye think I am?"

"Ye were thievin' my coos," he pointed out.

"Thievin' coos isn't the same as murderin' bairns."

"I'm not a bairn," one of the lads pronounced with indignation.

"I'm not a bairn," the other mimicked.

The man's furrowed brow softened fractionally, but his grip was still steel-hard.

What were his intentions? She shuddered to think. In some parts, cattle reivers were punished as severely as murderers.

"What do ye mean to do with me?" she challenged him, though her mouth was dry with fear as she spoke.

He didn't answer her. He only continued to stare at

her in silence while his flinty green eyes seemed to entertain a host of grim possibilities.

She nervously licked her lips, her mind racing. He obviously cared deeply for his sons. He was protective of them. She wondered...

"Ye wouldn't kill me in front o' *them,* would ye?" She glanced at the two lads, who were staying obediently back, but who still clung to their wooden swords. "Ye won't let them watch while their father slays a helpless lass."

It was a risky bluff. He might be the sort who wouldn't hesitate to demonstrate to his sons what happened to people who reived their father's cattle.

On the other hand, when he'd knocked her to the ground, he'd turned onto his shoulder to soften the blow. That proved he wasn't without mercy.

"Are ye goin' to slay her, Da?" one of the lads asked.

"Da wouldn't do that while she's unarmed," the other assured his brother. "'Twouldn't be chivalrous." Then he added, "He'll give her a sword. Right, Da?"

Cristy doubted that. Still, the lads' words had served to diminish the vengeful fury in their father's eyes. In fact, she would almost swear she saw a glimmer of amusement in his gaze as he let out his breath on a sigh.

A pounding footfall announced someone coming up the stairs from the lower level. Eager for any kind of distraction that might allow her to twist free, Cristy tossed the hair from her eyes to get a better look. Out of the shadows emerged a hefty woman with iron-gray hair, snapping eyes, and a heavy black skillet.

"All right!" she bellowed as she came. "Where's that connivin' cattle reiver? I'll give him such a wallop that he won't..."

The woman stopped in her tracks when she laid eyes on Cristy. She lowered the skillet, knitted her wiry brows, and then gasped. Handing the skillet off to the gray-haired man who'd answered the door, the woman rushed forward to peer down at Cristy. Her expression transformed swiftly from outrage to motherly concern and then back to outrage as she looked at Cristy's captor.

"What the devil are ye doin', m'laird?" the woman demanded.

Cristy's eyes widened. M'laird? Was this Macintosh himself?

"Can't ye see the poor lass is hurt?" the woman said, clucking her tongue.

Cristy almost choked in surprise. The last thing she expected from the skillet-wielding giantess was pity.

"Hurt?" Macintosh scoffed. "This is the lass who's been reivin' my cattle."

The woman bent forward to stare down at her with kindly eyes. "Was it ye who gave her that black eye then?"

"What?" He peered down at Cristy, apparently noticing her bruise for the first time.

It was tempting for Cristy to let everyone believe Macintosh had struck her, intentionally and cruelly. But she was reluctant to blame an innocent man for what her uncle had done.

Still, she wasn't stupid. She needed whatever advantage she could grasp.

"I'm sure ye didn't *mean* to do it," she hedged.

He wasn't fooled for an instant. "I didn't touch ye, lass, and ye know it. That's an old bruise."

The woman parked her hands on her hips. "Is that true, lass?"

Cristy caught her lip under her teeth, reluctant to answer. God only knew what Macintosh's punishment would be for reiving his cattle *and* lying to him.

Brochan shook his head. More than anything, he hated being blamed for things he hadn't done.

All his life, he'd followed the code of chivalry. He'd tried to be a decent man. He'd always done the honorable thing. He'd taught his sons right from wrong, leading by his example.

He had willingly and singlehandedly accepted responsibility for his children, his servants, a herd of cows, and this new holding with its derelict tower.

It was bad enough that anything that went awry was his fault. But to be accused of doing something as heinous and reprehensible as clouting a lass when he'd never dream of raising his hand to a woman...

"Da would never hit a lady," Colin said.

"Aye, thank ye, Colin." At least one person in this hall trusted his character. Brochan looked down at the bonnie reiver with smug satisfaction. "That's right."

Then Cambel added, "But sittin' on one is perfectly fine."

Rauf sounded like he was strangling on laughter.

Brochan sighed. The frankness of wee lads was both a blessing and a curse.

The lass beneath him arched her brow in challenge, awaiting his reply.

"Nay, Cambel," he admitted. "Sittin' on a lady is *not* perfectly fine. Not usually. But as laird, 'tis my duty to make sure she isn't goin' to hurt my clan."

"Why, Da? Is she dangerous?" Cambel asked.

He gazed down at his captive. *Was* she dangerous? He had her at his mercy now. But he had to admit, getting a closer look at the lass, that she was dangerously *attractive.* And between the feral beauty of her face, her arching bosom, and her insistent squirming between his thighs, the wee, wild wench was making him feel dangerously *awakened.*

"Is she, Da?" Colin echoed.

"Dangerous?" Brochan cocked his head at her. "Well, lass, are ye?"

"Ye'll find out just how dangerous if ye don't let me go."

Her words were harsh and threatening. But Brochan detected a flicker of fear in her eyes. He decided she was about as dangerous as a cornered kitten with tiny claws and her fur on end—all hiss and spit.

"I'd be a fool to let ye go," he told her gently. "But give me no trouble, and I'll do ye no harm. Once I get my cattle back, I'll return ye, good as new."

She looked horrified. "I'm a hostage?"

He winced. "I wouldn't say so much a hostage as a..." He couldn't really think of a better term.

"I'm a bloody hostage," she bit out, renewing her fight

to get free. "Ye son o' the devil!" She twisted beneath him. "Damn ye to hell!"

"Ooh! She's goin' to have to clean the garderobe, Da," Cambel announced.

"Aye," Colin agreed, telling the lass, "Da says if ye use foul words, ye have to do foul work."

If he weren't so busy battling the wee wildcat beneath him, Brochan would have grinned in approval at his sons' comments.

The lass's brown eyes smoldered with fury. "Let. Me. Go."

"What's a hostage, Da?" Colin asked.

"A hostage is someone you hold on to...for safekeeping," he said pointedly, "until the person who wants her back pays the price."

Cambel crept a bit closer. "What price?"

"Stay back, Cambel," he said. He didn't think the lass would hurt the lad, but he couldn't be sure. She seemed very desperate, despite his reassurances. "Her price is the five coos she stole from us."

"Who wants her back?" Colin asked.

"That's a very good question, Colin. How about it, lass? Whose clan do ye belong to?"

She froze for a heartbeat, and what he saw in her wide brown eyes spoke volumes. She didn't want to say.

"I don't belong to a clan," she lied.

She renewed her struggles, forcing Brochan to tighten his thighs around her. He sincerely wished she wouldn't do that. It was having an undesired effect, one he was sure she didn't intend.

"Ye had a whole gang o' lads with ye," he said. "I saw them."

"Could be the Moffats," Rauf suggested. "They own the adjoinin' property. There look to be five or six young men."

The reiver's brow creased, and Brochan could tell Rauf was right. "Are they your brothers then?"

She clamped her lips closed, obviously unwilling to say.

"Come on, lass," he reasoned. "If ye don't tell us, we won't be able to collect the ransom. Ye'll be stuck here."

"Ye can't keep me here," she said, adding with a sneer, "unless ye plan to sit on me all night."

That idea *did* sound pleasant to less honorable parts of his body, parts that hadn't been used in more than five years.

But he had other plans.

"That won't be necessary. I have shackles."

Mabel gasped, as if he'd said he was going to string the lass up by her braid.

Consequently, the lass, sensing an ally in Mabel, pressed her advantage. "Ye'd put me in shackles? Like a common criminal?"

"Damn it all! Ye *are* a common criminal," he argued, aroused and exasperated that he was aroused. "Ye were reivin' my bloody coos."

"Da!" Colin cried with glee. "Now *ye'll* have to clean the garderobe!"

Cristy half expected Macintosh to turn on his son and backhand him across the mouth for his impertinence.

That was what her uncle would have done. But the laird only muttered more oaths under his breath, mostly cursing himself.

Meanwhile, Cristy agonized over her predicament. It was bad enough that she'd been caught by the very man whose cow she'd been trying to steal, Laird Macintosh himself. But when her uncle found out...

Not only would she lose any hope of gaining his respect. She'd probably get a beating for her carelessness. She supposed it was no less than she deserved. But her cousins would never let her accompany them again.

She couldn't let that happen. She had to find a way to escape.

As much as she hated how helpless she felt, at the mercy of the self-satisfied brute—the way his hands dwarfed her wrists, how his eyes burned green fire, the unsettling weight of his body on top of her—she couldn't let him put her in shackles. Then she'd never be able to flee.

Perhaps it was in her best interests to go along with the laird after all. If she could get him to trust her, convince him she was harmless, maybe he would let down his guard. Then she could outwit him, escape, and return to the Moffat keep before morn.

Fighting all of her instincts, she relaxed beneath him, as if surrendering to his will.

She sighed, lowering her eyes. When she spoke, it was in the soft voice of defeat. "'Twasn't my idea to reive your coos, I swear."

The old woman took the bait at once. "Did they force ye, lass?" She clucked her tongue. "'Twas one o' them gave ye the black eye, wasn't it?"

Cristy nodded.

She felt the pressure on her wrists ease up the slightest bit.

"I knew it," the woman said. "'Twas those Moffat lads, aye?"

She nodded again.

When Macintosh spoke once more, his voice was gentle, compassionate...vulnerable. "What's your name, lass?"

"Cristy."

"And ye're a Moffat?"

"Aye." There was no use hiding her identity. Besides, honesty would serve to gain his trust. "They're not my brothers. They're my cousins."

As predicted, his grip on her loosened. "If I let ye up, ye won't do anythin' foolish, will ye?"

The temptation was great. But every scenario she ran through her head—lunging for the sword, elbowing back the old woman, diving for the door—ended with Macintosh back on top of her.

So instead, she obediently shook her head.

He released her cautiously, rocking back on his haunches. As if he'd read her mind, he immediately slid his sword across the rushes, far out of her reach.

He held out a hand to her. She resisted the urge to spit on his palm, instead taking his hand and allowing him to help her up. To her consternation, he didn't let go. And to her annoyance, his grip felt possessive and commanding.

"She's very bonnie," one of the lads said in a very loud whisper.

"Aye," whispered his brother.

"Lads," Macintosh warned them. Then he turned to his man. "Rauf, I'll write a missive to Moffat, demandin' the return o' my coos in exchange for his niece. Ye can send it with Brother William in the morn."

"Right," Rauf replied. "And I'll stand watch o'er the herd tonight, in case the Moffat lads return for the lass."

"Good." As Rauf headed outdoors, Macintosh nodded to the old woman. "Mabel?"

"M'laird?"

"Can ye see to the lads?"

"O' course. Are ye sure ye're..." The woman glanced at Cristy, as if she suspected Cristy might have mischief in mind.

Cristy *did* have mischief in mind. But she lowered her gaze and tried to appear suitably humbled.

"I'll be fine," Macintosh assured her. "But be sure and close the lads' chamber door."

"Kiss us, Da," one of them said.

"I'll come and kiss ye when ye're in your bed," the laird said.

For an instant, Cristy felt a pang in her heart. She couldn't remember the last time anyone had kissed her goodnight.

"Goodnight, bonnie lady," the other lad called from the stairwell.

Caught completely off-guard, Cristy mumbled back, "Goodnight."

Hand-in-hand with Mabel, the lads climbed the stairs, disappearing into the dark.

And then there were just the two of them in the great hall.

Now that she could get a good look at the laird, she realized how tall and formidable he was. He stood a full head above her, and his shoulders were nearly as wide as a doorway. It must have taken yards of linen to make a leine broad enough to span his chest.

"Cristy, is it?" he asked.

She nodded.

"Ye can call me Brochan."

"Brochan."

"Aye."

He was still holding her hand. It felt very improper now. With the casual air of a courting gentleman, he escorted her across the hall, stopping in front of a great cupboard.

"Listen, Cristy, I don't want ye to fret." He gave her hand what was probably supposed to be a comforting pat. "I truly mean ye no harm."

It took all of Cristy's willpower to appear docile and obedient, resisting the urge to snatch back her hand.

Until he opened the cupboard door and pulled out the shackles.

CHAPTER 4

Brochan hadn't been fooled for a moment by the lass's meek and mild behavior. She might appear to be tamed. But he'd seen the intrigue seething behind her innocent eyes.

He'd raised twin sons, after all. He'd encountered every manipulation known to man.

As predicted, once she saw the shackles, she began screaming in fury.

But he was prepared for her resistance. And now that his sons were safely upstairs, behind a closed door, he could ignore her screams. While she tugged back frantically on her captured hand and batted at him with her free one, he simply bent down and slipped one of the shackles around her ankle.

Then he lifted up the wee cursing lass, carried her to the hearth, and clapped the other shackle around the heavy iron fireplace crane.

"I may be kindhearted," he told her, "but I'm not a fool."

He gave the long, thick chain between the shackles a shake, testing its strength. Then he removed all the fireplace tools she might consider using as weapons.

While she called him every foul name he'd ever heard, he returned to the cupboard for a chamber pot. From the oak chest against the wall, he pulled out several thick sheepskins.

She was practically hoarse from screaming by the time he dumped her amenities beside her.

"Now ye have a choice," he said between her curses. "Ye can either stop your squallin', or I can fetch a gag to stuff betwixt your teeth. So what'll it be?"

That stopped her cries. But her dark eyes contained such smoldering hatred that he almost felt singed by her glare. Her hands were curled into tight fists. Her jaw was clenched as tight as a cockle. And her whole body heaved with the passion of her anger.

For a brief moment, he thought it was a shame she was so full of fury. She was actually quite a lovely lass. Her hair was as black as night, and the tendrils that had come loose from her long braid curled gracefully over her shoulders. Her eyes matched her woolen kirtle—a deep, rich brown, like the color of a brook trout in a shadowy loch. Her skin looked as smooth and sun-kissed as honey, and her lips were a soft, inviting pink.

In the next moment, her dark bruise caught his eye, and he wondered what kind of heartless brute would clout such a bonnie lass across the face.

Then he realized it was none of his affair. His hands were too full, raising his own lads, to be concerned with

how the Moffats treated their cousin. Even if he did feel sorry for the lass.

Nodding to approve her choice of silence, he returned to the cupboard for a sheet of vellum, ink, and a quill. Then he sat at the trestle table.

"Your uncle's name?" he asked, dipping the quill.

She glared at him in silence. The lass was decidedly more stubborn than his sons.

"Fine. Ye have another choice to make. Ye can either tell me, I'll write the missive, and then I'll leave ye in peace," he said, "or I can stay here, waitin', until ye feel the need to use the chamber pot. Maybe then ye'll tell me."

She glowered at him in disgust. "Douglas," she spat.

He wrote. "To Laird…Douglas…Moffat."

While he finished penning his demand, Cristy arranged the sheepskins to her liking and flounced down upon them, deliberately facing away from him.

He picked up the candle on the trestle table.

"Goodnight, Cristy. I'll send this out at dawn. If all goes well, Moffat will return my coos, and ye'll be back home, safe and sound, by midday."

She didn't answer him, but he doubted she was asleep. As vexed as she was, she'd probably toss and turn half the night before she finally drifted off.

Carrying the candle, he started toward the stairs. He'd promised his sons a goodnight kiss. It was something the lads insisted upon. And he was glad to do it. One day, they'd grow too old for the ritual. And he'd miss it.

As curious as it was, when he passed by the lass, he was tempted to stop and give her a kiss as well. She might be fierce and angry, but he sensed that beneath the surface, there was something vulnerable, some sad, neglected part of her that was starved for affection.

Again, it was not his affair. He couldn't save every small, suffering creature that crossed his path. He had too many other things to look after.

Colin and Cambel were sleeping back-to-back in their big bed when he eased open their chamber door. It was still odd to him that strangers couldn't tell the difference between the lads. To Brochan, they were as different as night and day.

The stars shone through the narrow window. It was a balmy evening, so he left the shutters open and banked the coals of the fire.

When he bent down to press his lips to Colin's brow, he suddenly remembered the comet. He glanced out the window, but it wasn't visible from here. He'd have to take the lads out to see it on the morrow.

He leaned over farther to kiss Cambel's brow. And it was then he recalled the tavern wench's prophecy.

She'd told him he could change his *stars* tonight. Was it just a coincidence that she'd chosen that word? Or was it possible she'd seen the comet as well?

It was accepted knowledge that comets foretold change. Brochan didn't really believe that. But it was admittedly eerie to have a tavern wench predict that his destiny would hang in the balance, this night of all nights, when a stranger had just entered his life.

Cristy thumbed away the stupid tear trickling down her cheek and gazed into the blurry flames on the hearth. There was no use in weeping. There was naught she could do now to change what had happened. Or what was going to happen.

Brochan Macintosh was going to get his cows back. What other choice did the Moffats have but to return them?

Her uncle would be furious. Her cousins would be disappointed. She was dreading their banishment almost more than the beating Douglas Moffat would give her.

After Macintosh had headed upstairs, she'd tried to free herself. She'd struggled with the shackle until her already twisted ankle was scraped raw. But it was no use. She couldn't escape.

She supposed it could be worse. Macintosh could have run her through with a sword. He could have hanged her. He could have decided to keep her prisoner. At least he was willing to ransom her.

And it wasn't so terrible here. He'd given her sheepskins to lie on. They were softer and warmer than the scratchy wool coverlet she used at home. The fire was pleasant, though the summer air was mild enough not to need its warmth. And he'd left her a chamber pot.

She rolled onto her back and peered around the great hall. It looked a bit unkempt. But he'd only lived here a short while. And it appeared his only servants were the pair he'd called Rauf and Mabel. With so few inhabitants, it was no wonder her cousins had been able to steal his cattle so easily.

The Moffat clan had at least a dozen servants, and four alone were in charge of the cows—two lads to watch over them and two maids to milk them each day and night. How Macintosh managed to keep track of his herd, which was double the size of theirs, she didn't know.

Maybe his sons worked in the field. They were young, but they seemed clever enough to watch over cows.

She'd never seen two lads who looked so alike, with matching russet hair and freckled noses. They must be twins. She'd never seen twins before. She wondered if Macintosh ever got them confused.

One of the wee lads had said Cristy was bonnie.

She smirked. Nobody ever said that about her. Her hair was too black. Her eyes were too fierce. Her skin was too dark. Obviously, the lad hadn't seen many lasses.

She wondered where the lads' mother was. Since the old woman had put them to bed, maybe their mother was dead like hers.

They were lucky at least to have a father—a father who kissed them goodnight and taught them not to curse and would brave the edge of a sword to protect them.

She gazed into the slowly dying fire, watching the flames double and blur as moisture again filled her eyes.

Despite the fact he'd lain awake half the night, Brochan rose at dawn, as he did every morn. And as usual, he scrubbed the sleep from his eyes while mentally reviewing what he needed to do for the day.

First he'd wake Colin and Cambel and send them out

to milk the cows. Mabel would be up already, baking oatcakes. Rauf was supposed to help him rebuild the stone wall around the garden this morn, and Mabel had promised to see what she could salvage of the overgrown herbs there. Brochan also had to tally the payments his uncle owed to the local vendors, for the old man had neglected to pay for some of the goods and services he'd received in the last year.

Then there were the stores that needed to be tossed out—broken crockery, soured ale, mouse-riddled grain. Once that was done, he'd have to account for what remained and replace what was necessary to survive the winter. It was going to be a long day.

Sitting up and swinging his feet over the edge of the pallet, he scratched at his stubbled jaw and blinked against the rising sun.

All at once he remembered the lass.

Damn. His well-ordered day was going to be even longer. Before he did anything else, he had to get his cows back and return Cristy Moffat.

Fully alert now, he threw on his leine and trews and raked his hands back through his hair before descending the stairs.

When he came into the great hall, what he saw at the hearth took his breath away. And then it took his heart away.

Cristy Moffat—sprawled like a queen across a mountain of sheepskins, coverlets, and furs—was snoring blissfully away beside the fire. Tucked around her, fast asleep—one on the left, one on the right—were his sons.

His chest tightened with fear, seeing Colin and Cambel so close to the woman who'd come at him with a sword last night.

Then he looked at the tangle of coverlets and realized they belonged to his sons. They must have sneaked down sometime in the middle of the night. A thick knot lodged in his throat. The fact that the lads were curled up around the lass like orphan pups tugged painfully at his heart.

He heard Mabel coming up the kitchen stairs behind him.

She whispered, "Forgive me, m'laird. I didn't have the heart to disturb them. But I don't think she'd hurt the lads."

He nodded.

Then she stepped beside him and cocked her head at the sight. "I fear the wee things miss havin' a mother."

Brochan clenched his jaw. It wasn't the first time Mabel had brought up the subject. She nagged him at every opportunity about getting a mother for the lads. She seemed to think Brochan could easily solve the problem by just snapping up some convenient wench to be a mother to his sons. It didn't seem to occur to Mabel that the lass would also be his wife. And that Brochan would never find a wife to equal the one he'd had.

He murmured through clenched teeth, "Don't ye have breakfast to attend to?"

Her cheer undiminished, she replied, "Aye, and I've made a hearty frumenty for our guest. The poor thing looks half-starved."

Brochan scowled at Mabel as she wheeled merrily and scurried back downstairs to the kitchens.

Frumenty? The old woman never made frumenty for *him.*

And guest? Cristy Moffat was definitely not a guest. She'd said it herself. She was a hostage. Brochan needed to get his cows back, and she was simply the means to achieve that.

Still, as he leaned a shoulder against the wall and continued to watch the dozing threesome, he couldn't help but smile when the delicate lass emitted a decidedly unladylike snort. Colin raised his sleepy head once to check on her and then shut his eyes and snuggled closer against her hip. Cambel turned over in his sleep and draped an arm over her thighs.

Brochan felt the familiar burden of guilt settle onto his shoulders. Was Mabel right to nag him? Was he being cruel to his sons by not remarrying? Were they hungry for maternal affection?

He perused the lovely lass. Could he be happy with someone like her?

Of course, no one would ever compare to his dear departed wife. And certainly a lass who reived cattle was not the sort of woman a proper laird should wed.

Contrary to what Mabel had said, the lass didn't look half-starved. She had a gently rounded bosom and a small waist, and where she'd kicked off the covers, her dark chestnut skirts had slipped up to reveal long, graceful legs.

Then his gaze lowered to the shackle he'd fastened around her ankle. He scowled, pushing off from the wall in concern. The skin around the iron ring was broken and

bloody. She must have tried to squeeze out of it.

He couldn't understand why. After all, he'd assured her he didn't intend to hurt her. He'd shown her kindness and mercy. He'd promised to return her as soon as he had his cattle. Why should she be so determined to escape?

Then he remembered that someone had given her that black eye.

While he was pondering all of that, she must have stirred. When he lifted his gaze again, she was staring at him. He wondered how long she'd been awake.

Startled, he blurted out the first thing that came to mind. "Did ye sleep well?"

He could have cursed himself for asking such a thing. Of course, she hadn't slept well. She was a hostage. She was lying on the floor of a stranger's great hall. Her ankle was bloody. And she was serving as a pillow for two presumptuous five-year-olds.

She must have agreed it was an inane question, because she didn't reply. And when she rose up on her elbows and frowned down at Colin and Cambel, Brochan panicked for one brief instant as he realized she could easily wrap the shackle chain around one of the lads' throats.

But she didn't seem vexed or violent. Instead, she appeared puzzled. And when she moved to sit up, the lads woke.

Eager to defuse the volatile situation, Brochan motioned to his sons. "Wake up, lads. 'Tis past time to milk the coos."

Cambel apparently felt he had to explain the circumstances. "We were worried about m'lady, Da."

"We didn't want her to get cold," Colin said, discreetly pulling Cristy's skirts back down over her legs to protect her modesty.

It took all Brochan's willpower not to grin at his son's gentlemanly gesture.

Brochan cleared his throat. "I'm sure she appreciates your concern, lads. But I fear a couple o' coos need some attention as well. Be off with ye. They'll be lowin' soon if ye don't tend to them."

The lads jumped up and, without even fetching their boots, scrambled out the door.

As they did, Mabel arrived with a steaming bowl of frumenty. "Ah, ye're awake. Here, lass," she said, passing by Brochan to deliver the breakfast. "This should warm your bones and put a wee bit o' meat on ye."

Cristy licked her lips as she looked at the bowl. Maybe Mabel was right. Maybe the lass *was* half-starved.

With a quiet word of thanks, Cristy dove into the bowl of oats, cream, berries, and spices as if it were the food of the gods.

Mabel seemed pleased. "'Tis my own grandma's recipe, passed down to me by my ma." She confided with a wink, "The secret is a wee bit o' honey."

As Mabel continued to expound on her grandmother's formula to their guest—their *hostage*, he corrected— Brochan couldn't help but wonder where *his* frumenty was.

Then he realized he really didn't have time for frumenty. He already had too much to do today, and this whole ransom situation had thrown an extra cog into his normally smooth-running mill.

"Did Rauf give the missive to Brother William?" he asked Mabel.

"Aye, m'laird. He said he saw neither hide nor hair o' the Moffat lads last night. So he sent your letter on to the laird with the monk. I've put Rauf to bed now so he'll be rested to help ye later today."

Brochan nodded tersely. He'd forgotten that after being on watch all night, his man would need to sleep. That meant Brochan's work was going to take that much longer. He definitely didn't have time to break his fast.

"Hopefully Rauf will be up and around by the time the coos come home," he said, thinking aloud. "I could definitely use an extra pair o' hands today."

"Well, he's an old man," Mabel admitted. "He needs his rest." And then, as if the brilliant notion suddenly occurred to her, she said brightly, "But as long as she's here, why not have the lass lend a hand? I'm sure she has some sort o' valuable household skills."

Irritated by Mabel's poorly disguised attempt at pointing out the lass's wifely talents and peeved at having to miss breakfast, Brochan muttered, "Ye mean other than reivin' cattle?"

CHAPTER 5

Cristy supposed he had every right to say that. But it hit a nerve.

Her uncle always said she was useless.

Cristy wasn't useless.

"Fie, m'laird!" Mabel protested. "O' course. Surely she can churn butter and shell peas," she suggested. "Och, and mend the lads' trews. Can't ye, lass?"

A child could do those things. Cristy suspected she was being flattered into menial labor. Nevertheless, her pride and boredom made her reply, "O' course."

"Excellent!" Mabel cheered with far too much enthusiasm. "I'll just take that bowl if ye're finished and bring a needle and thread."

Cristy could have eaten another bowl of the frumenty. It was the best thing she'd tasted in weeks. Her uncle never served such tasty fare. He had rather simple tastes and preferred oatcakes and watered ale to break his fast.

Mabel took the bowl and hurried down the stairs, leaving her alone with Macintosh.

He looked rather different in the light of day— younger and less menacing. She realized he wasn't much older than her. His sleep-mussed, chestnut-colored hair made him look as boyish as his sons. And though his eyes were shadowed from lack of sleep, she could see they were gentle and kind, just like Colin's and Cambel's.

"The missive should be delivered soon," Macintosh assured her. "Ye won't have to spend the whole day mendin' the lads' trews."

She nodded, though now that she'd passed a night unscathed in the house of the enemy, she wasn't particularly looking forward to going home. Naught awaited her there except her uncle's cruel tongue and hard knuckles.

She shrugged and said pointedly, "'Tis the least I can do to thank your *sons* for their charity."

He could not have missed her point. But he managed a smile anyway. And she was struck by the warmth in his face in spite of her sarcasm.

"I'm not certain ye should thank them for accostin' ye in the middle o' the night and stealin' half the covers," he said. "But I'm sure they had good intentions."

The truth was she hadn't minded them at all. When she'd first awakened in the middle of the night to hear the lads' worried whispers in the dark hall, something had melted inside her. When they threw coverlets over her shoulders and nuzzled against her, she'd never felt so cared for and so needed. A tiny part of her wished she could spirit the sweet lads away with her.

Of course, stealing Macintosh's lads would be far worse than reiving his cattle. She could see that he loved them more than life. Besides, he needed them here. With so few servants, someone had to milk the cows.

Brochan's brow furrowed briefly, and he went to the cupboard. Opening the door, he ran a finger along a shelf of small clay jars, stopping and taking one down. Then he came to hunker down beside her and gave her the jar.

"Healin' unguent," he explained, nodding to her ankle, "for your..."

He locked gazes with her, and her breath caught. This close, she could see his face clearly for the first time. Not only were his eyes the most beautiful and startling shade of rich green, but they were deep and expressive. In a single glance, she could see the whole history of his emotions written there—joy, grief, humor, hurt, strength, love.

Suddenly disarmed, she was at a loss for words. He seemed to be tongue-tied as well. But when his gaze lowered to her mouth, her heart made a queer flutter in her breast.

Before Cristy could wonder what was happening, Mabel came stomping up the stairs. Brochan moved away as fast as a spooked cow.

"I'm goin' to the garden now," he announced, his voice cracking over the words. "I've got to repair the wall."

"Aye, fine, m'laird," Mabel sang. "Don't ye worry about our wee guest. I'll keep her properly occupied."

Cristy watched him leave, seeing him with new eyes.

The young laird seemed to bear the whole weight of the world on his shoulders. And yet he still had room left in his heart to care for his sons and to make sure his hostage was comfortable.

She felt bad about stealing his cows now. And she was glad he was her neighbor. The old Laird Macintosh had been a sour and miserable man. This new laird seemed good-natured.

As Mabel handed her a pair of torn trews and tools to sew them, a silly hope sidled into Cristy's mind. Perhaps, after all this mess with his cattle was straightened out, she would come and visit on occasion. She liked Colin and Cambel. And she could even lend a hand to Brochan, just until he got his keep in order.

The lads returned an hour later, as she was taking the last stitch in Cambel's trews. At Mabel's prompting, they thanked Cristy, whom they insisted on calling m'lady, and dutifully took the trews and the coverlets they'd dragged down the stairs back up to their own chamber.

When they returned, they'd changed into the repaired trews. Mabel gave them each a couple of oatcakes and cups of fresh, warm milk. Colin insisted on sharing his milk with Cristy, boasting that he'd milked the cow himself. So she obliged him with a sip, though it was a strange taste to her, since she was much more accustomed to ale.

Mabel brought out the full butter churn and a basket of peas, returning to the kitchens to start the supper pottage. The lads took turns churning the cream, while Cristy shelled peas into a wooden bowl. It was soothing work, and the lads were good company.

They chatted about their old home, how there had been more kin living in the keep, but that they liked this big empty tower house because it was all theirs. Colin especially liked the cows. And Cambel enjoyed exploring, especially down by the burn.

Cristy told them she lived on the other side of that burn with her uncle. She explained that her parents were dead. And she learned from the lads that they'd never known their mother.

She asked them what it was like to have a brother who looked so much like them. They told her a few of the tricks they'd played on their kin. But they mostly found it disappointing that people couldn't tell them apart.

Cristy said she thought that was ridiculous, as ridiculous as not being able to tell cows apart. She assured them that even though she'd known them less than a day, already she could tell the difference between them. The lads brightened at that.

And then they began to ask more difficult questions.

Cambel stopped churning and wiped his brow. "Why did ye steal our da's coos, m'lady?"

Cristy almost dropped a peapod. How could she explain that?

She sighed. "'Twas a foolish trick, I suppose, maybe like the tricks ye played on your kin. I wanted to show off for my cousins."

"But stealin' is bad," Colin said.

"Aye."

"Are ye sorry?" Cambel asked.

"Aye."

"And are ye goin' to be punished?" Cambel asked.

"Probably."

"By our da?" Colin asked.

"Nay, by my uncle."

"What will he do?" Cambel asked.

Cristy didn't want to talk about it. She shrugged.

Cambel suggested to Colin, "Maybe he'll make her muck the stables."

Colin whispered back, "Mabel said Laird Moffat probably gave her the black eye. Maybe he'll hit her again."

Cambel straightened. "But that's not right. Da says ye should never hit a lady."

Cristy sighed. She was liking Brochan Macintosh more and more.

Colin took over Cambel's spot at the churn then, and Cambel added a block of peat to the fire.

"Do ye know any stories, m'lady?" Colin asked as he pumped the churn. "I like stories."

Cristy thought about it. Her mother had told her stories when she was a wee lass. One of her favorites was from the Bible—the tale of the shepherd David fighting the giant Goliath.

She regaled the lads with a rousing rendition of the battle, complete with a demonstration of David's sling, using a pod to fire a pea across the hall, which made the lads erupt in laughter.

"Will ye come back to visit us, m'lady?" Cambel asked.

"Aye, will ye?" Colin chimed in.

She was saved having to answer when the door

opened and Brochan returned from working outside. The lads leaped up and ran to him.

"Da!" Cambel cried. "Do ye know the story o' Goliath and wee David?"

"M'lady fixed my trews. See?" Colin turned his back and bent over so Brochan could view the mended seat of his trews, nearly splitting the seam again.

"We've been helpin' churn the butter."

"She can come visit us anytime, right, Da?"

"Lads, let me catch my breath," he told them.

Cristy could see Brochan was overwhelmed. He must have been working hard on the garden wall. He was dripping with sweat, and his forearms were smudged with mud. Yet he was still as aggravatingy handsome as the devil. And as tired as he must be, he had hugs and a smile for his sons.

"Mabel!" he called out. "Have ye got a spare ale?"

From the kitchens below, Mabel yelled, "Aye, be right up!"

Then his gaze fell on Cristy, and something caught in her throat. Brochan looked so content, standing there with an arm around each of his sons. She couldn't help but feel a sort of bittersweet envy.

Then Colin said exactly the wrong thing. "Ye aren't goin' to let m'lady go back to that bad man who beats her, are ye, Da?"

The awkward indecision in Brochan's eyes crushed her. Yet what could he say? All he knew about her was that she'd stolen his cows. What happened between her and her uncle wasn't his concern.

"Well...I..."

She came to his rescue. "I have to go home, Colin. But maybe I could come and visit now and then."

Brochan was clearly relieved. "Aye, if ye like. Would ye like that, lads?"

They jumped up and down and cheered.

Mabel came up the stairs with a tray of cups for everyone. "What's all this fuss?"

Colin replied, "M'lady is goin' to come and visit us."

"Is that so?"

Brochan clarified, "After the...situation...is resolved."

"No word yet?" Mabel asked, handing out the ales.

Brochan shook his head. "Ye're certain he gave the missive to Brother William this morn?"

"Och, aye. He said the monk was makin' rounds today, reassurin' the folk who were frettin' o'er the star last night."

"What star?" Colin asked.

"Och, lads," Brochan said, "I must show ye the star tonight. 'Tis a special star with a tail, called a comet. 'Tis quite spectacular."

So it hadn't been a dream, Cristy thought. The strange star was real. She'd begun to wonder if she'd imagined it.

"Can m'lady come see it with us?" asked Cambel.

"Well...Miss Moffat is most likely goin' home today," Brochan explained.

The lads' faces fell, and Cristy had to admit she felt the same disappointment.

"That's all right," she told them, "I've seen the star already."

"That's right, ye have," Brochan said, no doubt remembering that her distraction by the comet was how he'd been lucky enough to catch her.

"If ye wash up, I can bring us all pottage," Mabel said.

Brochan shook his head. "I just came in for an ale. I'm only half done with the wall. Is Rauf up and around yet?"

"Nay, m'laird, and 'twill be a while. Don't ye have accounts to go over? Why don't ye come sup with us now and do your outdoor work later? Rauf can help ye finish the wall this afternoon."

Brochan rubbed the back of his neck, considering the idea. Cristy was astounded that he was hesitating. He hadn't broken his fast, as far as she'd seen. Did the man take no time to eat?

Mabel said, "Ye can bring your work to the table, slay two birds with one stone."

"One stone?" Colin tugged on Brochan's trews. "That's just like David, Da."

"I suppose 'tis." Brochan smiled and ruffled his son's hair. "Fine. I'll go wash up. But I'm countin' on ye lads to help me with the accounts."

When he returned and Mabel began to serve supper at the table, the lads made more trouble.

"Da," Cambel whispered, just loud enough for Cristy to hear, "we can't make m'lady sit on the floor to eat."

"Aye," Colin agreed. "'Tis unchivalrous."

"Can't ye take off her chains?" Cambel asked.

Brochan replied in a murmur. "Lads, she's our prisoner. If we let her escape, she'll go home, and we'll never get our coos back."

Cristy stared into the fire, pretending not to hear, though she was hanging on every word. Would they unshackle her? Was escape still possible?

Colin tried to convince Cambel. "Da's right, Cambel. We have to get our coos back."

"But 'tis dishonorable," Cambel argued. He frowned and crossed his arms over his chest. "I won't eat my pottage unless she's allowed at the table."

Cristy feared Cambel was begging to be clouted for his impertinence. But Brochan answered him with patience and consideration.

"Indeed?" he said. "Then what would ye suggest?"

"I know," Colin said. "She could give us her word she won't flee."

"Her word?" Brochan almost choked. "And how do ye know ye can trust her word?"

"She's a lady," Cambel said, as if it were obvious.

Brochan smirked. "Ye've much to learn, lads. But if ye think 'tis the right thing..."

Cristy's pulse raced.

Colin and Cambel answered in unison, "Aye."

Brochan went to the cupboard and brought back a key. He dropped to one knee beside her. "Do ye swear ye won't try to escape?"

"Aye."

"Do ye give the lads your word on it?"

"Aye."

He sprang the shackle and held out a hand to help her up. For one tense instant, she thought about racing for the door, despite her oath. And as if he read her mind, he clasped her hand firmly in his and led her to the table, wedging her strategically between his two sons, to whom she'd just given her solemn word.

The pea and barley pottage Mabel served in a crust of coarse maslin was just as delicious as the frumenty. Cristy thought she'd be glad of an excuse to visit every day if the food was always so appetizing.

While they ate, Brochan looked over several documents he'd brought to the table. Then he slipped a page toward the lads and asked them to recite the numbers in a long column while he checked them off on another page.

Cristy was astonished the young lads could decipher the marks on the page. She wished she could. Women were seldom tasked with anything requiring such knowledge. But she often wondered how much more power she would have if she could read and write.

In a flight of whimsy, Cristy imagined coming here every day to learn from the lads how to recognize numbers and pen letters.

When Brochan no longer needed the lads, Mabel put them to work, sweeping up the rushes on the floor of the great hall. The old woman said she planned to see what crops she could salvage from the overgrown garden.

Meanwhile, she quietly brought a ripped leine to the table and asked Cristy if she wouldn't mind mending it.

Brochan glanced up. "That's *my* leine," he murmured to Cristy. "Ye don't have to do it."

"I don't mind," Cristy said. Otherwise, she'd be bored,

with naught to do. "I promise I won't even sew the sleeves shut."

He snorted at that.

The afternoon was the most peaceful Cristy had passed in a long while. Between the fire crackling on the hearth, the laird quietly scrawling figures, the whispery sweep of the rushes, and the soothing repetition of stitching, she felt calm and restful.

She'd just made a final knot in the thread when she glanced up to see Brochan slumped atop the table. His pen was still in his hand. His head rested on his forearm. And his open mouth was making a soft sawing sound. She smiled. He looked more like his sons than ever when he was asleep.

All at once, a dangerous thought occurred to her. Mabel was outside. Rauf was in his chamber. Brochan was asleep. And she was no longer shackled. She could easily send the lads on some errand upstairs and slip out the door. Her heart raced as she considered the possibility.

Then she thought about Mabel, who had made her a bowl of frumenty and treated her like a guest. She glanced again at the poor overworked laird dozing on the table. She watched his kind and dutiful sons, piling rushes near the door.

She'd given them her word. She'd promised she wouldn't flee. And though it might mean a beating for her if she didn't escape, she couldn't stomach the thought of betraying the sweet lads. Or their father.

So, silently cursing herself for a fool, she carefully set

his mended leine aside so as not to wake the laird. Then she glanced around the hall, wondering what else she could do to make herself useful.

Brochan woke to the sound of Rauf coming downstairs. Startled and disoriented, the laird lifted his head, nearly upsetting the vial of ink. Then he frowned and gave his head a good shake, dispelling the fog from his brain.

Had he fallen asleep at his work? Again?

He had to stop that. There was too much to do for the luxury of dozing.

The rushes were gone from the great hall. The lads must have finished their chores. But where were they now? And Cristy...

His blood turned to ice as he realized the lass was missing. He stood up, knocking the bench over with a great thud.

"M'laird, what's wrong?" Rauf said as he stepped into the hall.

"Where is she? Where is the Moffat lass?"

Rauf looked befuddled. "I've only just awakened, m'laird. I thought she'd be ransomed by now. Do ye want me to look for her?"

Brochan was too troubled to answer. This was his fault. His lads were missing, and his hostage was gone. He should never have trusted the word of a reiver.

With his heart in his throat, he strode toward the door.

It swung open before he could reach it. In came Colin,

Cambel, and the lass, their arms overloaded with great clumps of sweet-smelling green rushes.

Unable to see where she was going, Cristy barreled forward and collided with him, dropping rushes everywhere. She would have fallen backwards from the impact, but he reached out and seized her elbow to steady her.

"Da! Ye're awake!" Colin called as he dropped his rushes.

Cambel dropped his as well. "M'lady took us to cut new rushes. See?"

It was then he noticed that Cristy was holding a scythe, the scythe he kept by the front door. He narrowed his gaze. Last night she would have tried to use the thing to cut him off at the knees.

But today when he looked at her, the smoldering hatred he'd seen in her face before was gone. Her dark eyes danced with delight. And her wide smile revealed beautiful white teeth. Colin was right. She *was* a bonnie lass.

Apparently, the bonnie lass had kept her word. She hadn't kidnapped his sons after all.

"Well, Da?" Cambel asked. "Are ye goin' to give m'lady a proper thank ye?"

He was standing close enough to her that he could see the pink kiss of the sun across the bridge of her nose and smell the fresh summer air on her loose hair. As his gaze fell to the gentle upward curve of her lips, he was sorely tempted to give her an *im*proper thank you.

The thought was disturbing. In five years, he'd

thought of no one in that way. He'd clung to the memory of his wife, remembering her touch, her embrace, her kiss. That he was daydreaming about kissing another woman troubled him.

So he set her at arm's length and gave her a nod of gratitude. "Thank ye, m'lady."

Rauf stepped forward then, clearing his throat. "If ye're ready to take a look at that garden wall, m'laird..."

"Aye," Brochan said, eager to evade temptation. "I can come back to the accounts later. I've got the wall halfway done, and I want to finish before dark."

"Then when 'tis dark," Colin told Rauf, "we're all goin' out to see the great comet."

"Are we?" Rauf raised a brow at Brochan.

Brochan shrugged. "I promised the lads I'd take them out."

"And m'lady is comin' as well," added Cambel.

Rauf's brow lifted even higher.

"We'll see, Cambel," Brochan said. "Her laird is likely worried about her and will send for her soon."

As it turned out, Moffat must not have been very worried about his neice after all. He sent neither the cows nor a message back with the monk. Brother William passed by on his way home, taking a moment to admire the newly repaired garden wall. But though he assured Brochan he'd delivered the missive into the laird's hands himself, he reported that Moffat had simply scoffed and sent him on his way.

Brochan was glad Cristy wasn't around to hear that. It would no doubt break her heart. But then he guessed that a man who considered it acceptable to strike a woman might also think it acceptable to torment her by delaying her ransom. And that thought made him feel ill.

So he penned another demand to send with the monk, this one a bit more threatening. For each day of delay, Brochan would add one cow to the price of Cristy's return. Surely that would get Moffat's attention.

Later, when Cristy asked if there was news from her uncle, he told her that Moffat was negotiating fiercely for her return, but that Brochan didn't feel he was offering what she was worth.

She seemed mildly disappointed. No doubt she expected Moffat to return the cattle at once to ensure her safe return, not to negotiate for a lower price. But Brochan was glad he hadn't told her the truth. It would have crushed her.

When it began to grow dark, Mabel announced that she and Cristy had a surprise for everyone. Brochan shook his head in amusement. He hadn't seen the old woman so full of life in a long time. Apparently, she was intent on impressing their "guest." He'd heard the busy clattering of pots and pans from upstairs when he sent the lads out for the late milking. Now, as he sat finishing up the accounts by candlelight, he smelled the savory aroma of something baking in the kitchens.

What the ladies had planned was dinner under the stars on the crest of the motte surrounding the tower house. From there, they could view the heavens in all their splendor, as well as keep an eye on the herd below.

Rauf spread a wool cloth on the grass for them to sit

on. Of course, the lads had to squeeze in beside Cristy. Under the evening sky, they dined on flaky pork coffyns, oatcakes spread with soft ruayn cheese, and crispels with cloudberries. Mabel said that Cristy had found a dusty-shouldered bottle of Port in the corner of the buttery, so she poured everyone a cup, even giving the lads a few drops.

The sky darkened until the stars popped out, one by one. Then Brochan pointed out the comet near the horizon to the lads.

"See how it has a long tail streamin' out behind it?"

"Why does it have a tail?" Cambel asked.

Colin asked, "Where is it goin', Da?"

"Is it goin' to crash into the earth?"

"Are the coos afraid of it?"

Brochan chuckled. "The coos don't *seem* afraid of it. Do ye think they are?"

"Nay," Colin decided.

Mabel added, "Some *folks* are afraid of it."

"Why?" asked Cambel.

"They say such a star can bring bad weather or bad luck," Mabel said.

"What do ye think, Da?" asked Colin.

Brochan frowned. "I don't think a faraway star, way up in the sky, can do us any harm down here."

"What about ye, m'lady?" Cambel asked. "Do ye think it brings bad luck?"

Brochan nearly spat out his oatcake. The star had certainly brought Cristy bad luck. If she hadn't been staring at it, he wouldn't have caught her so easily.

But Cristy sounded pensive. "I'm not sure." And when she continued, her words echoed what the tavern wench had said. "I've heard the star has the power to change one's fate. But I don't know if 'tis good or bad."

"I think 'tis good," Cambel declared. "After all, the star brought ye to us, m'lady."

Brochan saw him give her a squeeze of affection, and his heart pinched at the gesture.

"'Tis a very kind thing to say, Cambel," she replied.

"I think so too," Colin said, not wishing to be excluded.

She gave him a hug as well.

Brochan didn't know what to say about that. He was fairly certain what had brought Cristy to them was not the star, but a cattle reiving gone awry.

Nevertheless, the night felt magical as they continued to watch the heavens and the unique star perched in the sky. Somewhere deep in his heart, Brochan made a wish—a secret wish on the star—that he could always feel this content.

CHAPTER 6

When Brochan rose the next morn, he was sure he'd find his sons tucked around the reiver lass again. He'd heard them last night when they thought he was asleep, stealing down the stairs and dragging their coverlets with them.

He should probably have stopped them. After all, it would serve no purpose to let them get close to her. It would only make it all that much harder for them when she left.

But he didn't have the heart to call them back. And in truth, he envied their daring. He wished he could creep down and crawl under the furs with the lass.

Mentally chiding himself for such reprehensible thoughts, he continued down the steps. But when he entered the great hall, fragrant now with fresh, sweet rushes, the coverlets were stacked neatly away, and the hearth was deserted.

Where were his sons? Where was his hostage?

Unwilling to resort to premature panic, Brochan descended to the kitchens to find Mabel.

"Good morn, m'laird," she sang out.

"Where have the lads gone?"

"Och, they've taken Cristy out to milk the coos."

He let out an invisible sigh of relief. Then he blinked. The lads rarely got up before dawn. Perhaps having a guest was giving them a sense of responsibility.

The scent of warm cinnamon was making his mouth water. He nodded to a tray full of freshly-made pastries. "What are these?"

"Almond frytours."

He reached out to take one, and she gave his hand a smack. "They're for supper, a special treat for Cristy."

He scowled. "Ye've never made these for *me*."

She told him matter-of-factly, "Well, honestly, m'laird, ye've never seemed to care if ye were eatin' capercaillie or collops."

He raised his brows. Was that true? He supposed he hadn't expressed much interest lately in what he put in his mouth, as long as it filled his belly. Half the time he was too busy or tired to eat. The other half, he shoved down his food as fast as possible so he could get back to work.

He furrowed his forehead in disappointment.

"Och, here," Mabel said, looking sorry for him. She handed him a couple of frytours and poured him a cup of watered ale. "I'll make up another batch."

He returned to the great hall to eat, mentally reviewing his tasks for the day. The frytours *were* delicious. Perhaps he should tell Mabel so. Perhaps then she'd make them more often.

Now that he'd figured out how much he owed to the various vendors, he had to count out the silver and send Rauf to deliver the payments. Mabel said she'd accompany Rauf so she could purchase food supplies. While she was away, Brochan planned to clear out the goods in the pantry that were beyond use. And with any luck, sometime today Moffat would arrive with the Macintosh cattle to exchange for his niece.

By the time he finished counting out the payments he owed and enclosing them in pouches with the receipts for Rauf, the sun was already streaming in to the hall. He wondered what was taking the lads so long. He could use their help today, sealing cracks in the dovecot. He'd promised Colin he could keep chickens, but first he had to make sure the dovecot was in good repair.

When he wandered outside, the cows had already been milked. The wooden buckets were brimming, and the pair of milk cows were ambling slowly back toward the rest of the cattle. But where were Colin and Cambel?

Shielding his eyes with his forearm, Brochan gazed down the slope.

In the midst of the herd, acting as if she was impervious to the great beasts, stood wee Cristy, as bold as a knight. She had Cambel and Colin with her.

Brochan's heart staggered. His sons never visited the cattle without his supervision. It was too dangerous. Cows were unpredictable, and they spooked easily. Did the lass know that? Did she understand cattle at all?

Shite.

His first instinct was to yell at them to get away from the herd. But he knew that would be a mistake. Naught would set off a stampede like a sudden loud bellow. He rubbed an anxious hand across his chin.

Where was the bull? Thankfully, at the other end of the field, peacefully chewing his cud.

But there were still several protective cows with young to worry about.

Moving as swiftly as he dared, he slipped down the brae.

What the devil was the lass thinking? Why had she let the lads wander into the thick of the herd? What was she doing?

God's eyes, he had neither the nerves nor the time for this.

Halfway down the slope, he slowed his pace. As he continued to watch, he realized what Cristy was up to as she held the lads' hands to keep them close, moving purposefully between the cows, herding them, isolating one from the rest.

Bloody hell. The mischievous minx was teaching his sons how to reive cattle.

"That's it," Cristy murmured. "Go slow enough not to spook her. But not so slow that she thinks ye're a wolf. Once she starts walkin' in the direction ye want, move with her so she keeps goin' forward, but keep your distance."

The lads did just as they were told. She was impressed. They were learning fast. She hadn't been much older than they were when she'd first learned to handle cattle.

They moved steadily alongside the cow until it was separated from the rest of the herd and walking at a good pace.

"Ye did it!" she quietly cheered. "If ye wanted, ye could walk her wherever ye liked now. She's—"

"Psst!"

Cristy jumped. Brochan had startled her, coming up behind her that way. But she didn't want to panic the cows, so she instructed the lads, "Just keep calm."

"What do ye think ye're doin'?" Brochan's voice was hushed, but she could feel the intensity of his anger in the bite of his words.

"Quiet, Da," Cambel warned.

"We're reivin' Eufemie," Colin whispered.

"I can see that," Brochan muttered.

Cristy, recognizing the impatience in his tone, suggested, "Why don't we put her back with the rest o' the herd now, lads?"

"But I want to take her to your keep," Cambel said.

Cristy arched a brow. "Now, Cambel, I told ye before—"

"Is that what ye intended?" Brochan said between clenched teeth. "Were ye goin' to reive my coo *and* my sons?"

Her jaw dropped. She stopped in her tracks, halting the two lads and the cow. Then she craned her head toward him. "How could ye think that?"

The dark fire in his eyes told her exactly how he could think that. He saw her only as a cattle reiver, a lass who'd attacked him with a sword and might be a threat to his sons, a lass who someone had given a black eye, and who probably deserved it.

The hurt she felt was unexpected. Normally, her skin was as thick as chain mail. It had to be. If she showed a hint of weakness, her cousins would swoop down on her like a hawk on a mouse. But to her horror, the accusation and condemnation in Brochan's gaze made her eyes well with moisture.

She tried to transform the hurt to anger, but her voice broke when she spoke. "I gave ye my word."

"Your word? The word of a..." He left the sentence unfinished, apparently not wishing to berate her in front of his sons. Then he looked away. His mouth was working as if he battled with his emotions.

Cristy steeled her chin, trying to still its trembling. She'd been so happy a moment ago, carefree and content, holding hands with two endearing children, playing in the sunshine, teaching them a useful skill.

Now she was good-for-naught Cristy the reiver again.

Colin and Cambel peered up at her. Colin spoke. "Are ye all right, m'lady?"

Cristy choked back the pain. Somehow she managed to nod. At least *someone* believed her. At least *someone* thought she was worthy of trust.

"We're all goin' back to the byre," Brochan proclaimed, his voice gruff. "There's to be no more reivin' o' cattle today."

"Och, Da," Cambel complained. "M'lady said we're good at it."

Brochan made a strangling sound deep in his throat.

"And Eufemie doesn't mind," Colin said.

"No more reivin'," Brochan insisted. "Ye lads know better."

Colin sighed. "I'm sorry, Da."

"I'm sorry, Da," echoed Cambel.

No one spoke on the way. The lads were still holding her hands when they reached the byre. And by then, Cristy's armor was back in place.

"Ye lads take the milk in to the house," Brochan said. "I need to speak with Miss Moffat alone."

Cristy's breath caught. She didn't want to let go of the lads. She knew once they were gone, Brochan would feel free to unleash his anger on her.

But if they disobeyed him, that anger might be unleashed on his sons.

Cristy could deal with a man's rage. She'd had plenty of practice. But she feared the lads didn't have such strong armor. So she gave them a forced smile of reassurance and reluctantly released them.

As soon as the twins were well on their way to the tower and out of hearing, Brochan turned on her. "What the devil were ye thinkin', endangerin' my sons like that?"

"They weren't in any danger."

"The hell they weren't." He started pacing. "There's a bull out there and coos with young. Do ye know what they'd do if they felt threatened?"

"Aye, o' course."

"Aye? Then why would ye take my lads out there?"

"God's bones! Do ye think I don't know cattle? I've been around them my whole life. I know how to stay out o' harm's way." Miffed, she added pointedly, "At least from coos."

Brochan stopped in front of her, and for an instant, she cursed her own waspish tongue, wondering if he would clout her after all. He might have told his sons that it wasn't right to hit a lady. But they weren't here to see him now.

Besides, it was obvious he didn't think she was a lady, not really.

He didn't hit her, but he did curse. "Shite. Teachin' my sons to be outlaws."

She creased her brow. Was that what he thought? No wonder he was angry. "What? I wasn't teachin' them to be outlaws."

"They were reivin' a bloody coo."

"'Twas their own bloody coo. They weren't reivin' her."

He let out an exasperated sigh. "'Twas Colin who put ye up to it, wasn't it? He wanted to know how to reive cattle."

Cristy stiffened. She wasn't about to let sweet wee Colin take the blame for it, even if that *had* been the lad's idea.

"'Twasn't his fault. 'Twas my idea. And I wasn't actually teachin' him how to reive cattle, only how to herd them." That much was true. Learning how to separate a single cow from the rest was a useful skill. "Don't hurt the lad."

"Hurt him?" He pulled away, aghast. "Ye think I would hurt Colin? My own flesh and blood?"

Cristy bit her lip and looked at him uncertainly. She was Douglas Moffat's own flesh and blood, and it didn't stop him from hurting her.

Brochan searched her face, shaking his head as if he were trying to figure out the strange workings of her mind. Then he reached out toward her hair.

Out of instinct, she flinched away.

Too late, she realized he didn't mean to clout her.

"Och, lass," he said in disbelief, his hand still raised, "are ye afraid o' me?"

She lifted her chin, putting on a brave face. "Nay."

But he didn't believe the lie. And the fact that he'd scared her made him look utterly crestfallen, so much like his wee sons that it squeezed her heart.

"Well," she amended, "ye *are* very angry."

He lowered his hand and stared down at his feet for a moment. "I *am* angry." Then he scoffed at himself. "I *was* angry." He lifted his head and locked gazes with her. His eyes were earnest and impassioned. "But I've never raised a hand in anger to my sons. And I would never, *ever* hurt a lady."

She gulped. Somehow in her heart she knew that. It was only habit that had made her duck away. Brochan was not at all like her kin. He was kind and noble and just.

He approached her again, this time with caution, as if she were a wild cat. "May I?" He lifted his hand, slowly.

His fingers in her hair were almost soothing as he

plucked out a stray piece of straw. Then he locked gazes with her.

She held her breath. She couldn't remember the last time a man had looked at her with such compassion or touched her with such tenderness. She felt herself drawn into the deep verdant pools of his eyes.

It was a wee bit frightening.

She'd worn invisible armor for years now. It served to protect her against her cousins' subtle cruelty. It might not be strong enough to ward off her uncle's fists, but it kept her safe from his demeaning words.

Now, the way Brochan was touching her with measured care, looking at her with affection and concern, it felt like he was gently stripping away that armor, link by link.

A new fear fluttered in her breast.

But it wasn't dread.

It was anticipation.

Her gaze fell to his mouth, and she couldn't help but wonder what it would be like to press her lips to his, to melt into his welcoming arms, to feel perfectly safe and protected.

She let out the breath she'd been holding. It came out on a tremble.

She was going to do it. She couldn't help herself. She was going to kiss him.

Brochan couldn't believe he was going to kiss her. Every instinct told him not to. No good would come of it. He could think of at least a dozen good reasons not to do such a reckless thing. And he would list them all...right after he finished the kiss.

Their attraction was as inevitable and unavoidable as the pull of steel to a magnet. The distance closed between them with natural grace. When their mouths met, it felt like coming home.

Her lips were soft, warm, and vulnerable as she pressed them tentatively against his mouth.

She was shaking. Perhaps she'd never kissed a man before. But since he hadn't kissed a woman in five years, he too was out of practice.

Yet instinct swiftly took over. He moved his hand to cup her silky cheek, drawing her closer. He closed his eyes, angling his head to capture her lips between his.

She responded with a soft gasp. She placed her hands on his chest—not to push him away, but to clench her fists in his leine.

The long-banked coal of his desire flickered to life.

He threaded his fingers through her silken hair. He circled her ear with the pad of his thumb, deepening the kiss.

She answered instantly, seeking out his mouth, striving to get even closer.

Encouraged by her response, he circled her waist with his other arm and drew her up against him. He groaned at the familiar and divine sensation of a woman's body pressed firmly to his—the supple yielding of her breasts upon his chest and the sweet curve of her hips below his palm.

Then she slipped her tongue out to taste him.

Like lightning striking dry grass, his passion flared to life. Hot blood raced through his veins as he opened his mouth, granting her access.

His tongue danced with hers, lightly at first and then with more devotion, and they sang the music of desire. Like a starving man, he feasted upon her, and she drank his greed as if it were wine.

Suddenly her hands were everywhere, skimming his chest, roving over his shoulders, weaving through his hair. He explored her beautiful contours as well, delving his fingers into her inky tresses, tracing her delicate throat with his fingertips, and venturing lower, daring to brush his palms atop the sensitive tops of her breasts.

The breath she raked in was so raw with need that he felt the surge in his trews like the powerful wave of a stormy sea.

All the lust that had been bottled up for the last five years streamed through his veins at once in a brilliant flare, blinding him to reason. He tore away from the kiss and nudged her up against the wall, wanting her so badly he could scarcely breathe.

Somewhere in the depths of his soul, he knew he was behaving like an animal. But what he glimpsed in her eyes wasn't pain or fear. It was a desire as strong and pure as his. She wanted him. She wanted this.

In another moment...

"Hallo!" he heard from outside the byre.

Cristy's eyes went wide.

Brochan stepped away, silently using every foul oath he could think of.

Curse Brother William. Naught could douse the flames of passion faster than the voice of a monk.

Yet Brochan's fire was far from extinguished. The evidence of his lingering desire displayed itself as proudly as a pennant pole in his trews. With a look at Cristy that was half apology, half exasperation, he turned his back to her, made the necessary adjustments, and prepared to face the monk.

"I'm in here, William."

As William entered the byre, Brochan suddenly remembered that the monk might have news that could upset Cristy.

He turned to her. "Will ye go see to the lads?"

She seemed glad of an excuse to leave, especially when she saw their visitor was a man of the church. She gave him a curt nod in greeting, picked up her skirts, and scurried off.

"Was that…" William began.

"Aye, Miss Moffat." He didn't feel like excusing his lack of an introduction…or detailing why they were alone in the byre…or explaining why the woman he was holding hostage apparently had free range of the property. "What news?"

"I've brought a missive from her laird," William said, handing over a small rolled parchment.

Brochan hesitated, stricken by an urge to destroy the thing without reading it. Part of him would rather leave things just as they were, with the lovely, sweet-lipped lass under his care.

But he was a man of honor. He'd offered a fair

exchange. He had to be true to his word.

So he popped the seal and opened the document.

On it were scrawled three words.

Keep her. Moffat.

Brochan kept staring at the letters. He couldn't be reading that right. There had to be some mistake.

But no matter how many times he read it, the message was as clear, raw, and brutal as it could be. He tightened his fist around the missive as rage slowly burned inside him.

"Is somethin' wrong, m'laird?"

Beyond speech, Brochan clenched his jaw and handed the parchment to the monk.

William frowned as he read the note. "I don't understand. 'Tis only five coos. Surely he wants the lass back."

Brochan's heart twisted with fury and sorrow. How could a man be so cruel? Did he truly value his cattle above his own niece? Was he so apathetic about the lass that he would casually cast her aside? What a monstrous man he must be.

"How will I tell her?" he wondered aloud. "How will I tell her her own uncle doesn't think she's worth five coos?"

William shook his head. "'Tis a travesty. She looks to be a lovely lass too. Most men would trade a whole herd o' cattle for a beauty like her."

Brochan had to agree. With her night-black hair and deep brown eyes, she was as bonnie and enticing as a dark faerie queen.

He rubbed his hand across his mouth, wondering how he was going to break the news to her. "Wait. What did ye just say?"

"I said she was a lovely lass."

"Nay, after that."

"Most men would trade a whole herd o' cattle for a lass like that."

"That's right. They would." Suddenly inspired, he snatched the missive from William's hand. Then he clapped his palm on the perplexed monk's shoulder. "Thank ye for takin' care o' this, William. I'm grateful for all ye've done."

After bidding the monk a hasty farewell, he headed toward the tower house. Halfway to the keep, he ripped the missive in half and tossed it away. By the time he reached the door, he'd weighed all the consequences and made up his mind.

It was completely reckless and irresponsible of him to keep Cristy in his home. His sons were growing too fond of her. Mabel was growing too fond of her. And *he* was growing too fond of her.

Cristy was a dangerous temptation. There was every reason to return her as soon as possible, whether or not he got his cows and whether or not her uncle wanted her back.

Keeping the peace between clans was the right thing to do. Holding on to her and risking a clan war with his own neighbor was rash and reckless.

Fortunately, Brochan didn't mind being rash and reckless.

CHAPTER 7

I t took all Cristy's willpower to keep up a calm appearance for the lads when her emotions were writhing around her brain in a tangled mess.

Kissing Brochan, she'd never felt so alive. One moment in his arms, and all her cares had vanished. He'd opened a locked chest inside her and revealed a treasure of new feelings.

It felt like a sultry wind had blown through her soul and awakened every fiber of her being. Yet within that sharp and wakeful clarity was a mist that softened the edges of reality, making it seem like the inside of a dream. Her sense of reason might be muted, but the rest of her senses had been heightened to dreamlike intensity.

Then that cursed monk had ruined everything.

In one moment, she'd felt like a warhorse primed to charge across the field.

In the next, she'd felt an abrupt backward pull on the reins, preventing her from moving.

And now she had to pretend that naught had happened, to speak to the wee lads as if she hadn't just been dallying with their father in the byre.

Colin shook his head. "I should never have asked ye to show us how to reive cattle," he said, his voice full of regret.

"And I should have protected ye," Cambel said ruefully. "Da says gentlemen are supposed to protect ladies."

Cristy gave them each a fond squeeze. But she was only half listening, trying to settle her rattled nerves with a cup of ale as she stared into the fire.

"What do ye think he'll do to us?" Colin asked his brother.

"He might make us scrub the chamber pots," Cambel gravely decided.

"Or pick up the coo pats," said Colin.

"Or wear stick tails," Cambel said with a shudder.

"What?" Cristy asked. What were the lads going on about?

"Once," Cambel said, "we tied a stick to a hound's tail for fun. Da tied stick tails onto our belts and made us wear them for two days."

"To shame us," Colin explained.

"Aye, to shame us."

Cristy blinked. If her uncle ever picked up a stick, it was to beat her.

"What about ye, m'lady? What do ye think he'll do to ye?" Colin wondered.

A dozen wildly inappropriate ideas popped into

Cristy's head, and she almost spat out her ale.

Cambel suggested, "Maybe she'll be rescued by her uncle before Da has a chance to punish her."

Cristy hoped not. After that blissful embrace, she'd be willing to clean chamber pots, pick up coo pats, *and* tie a stick around her waist just to see where that kiss would lead.

Still, the reminder that she didn't belong here was sobering. She wondered if the monk had brought news from her uncle. Was he going to return the cattle today?

"I don't want ye to go," Colin admitted.

"I don't want ye to go either," Cambel said, leaning against her thigh.

A lump lodged in her throat. She knew how they felt.

At that moment, Brochan came in, stomping the dirt from his boots at the door.

Cristy was afraid to look at him. She was afraid of what she might see in his eyes. What if the monk had brought bad news? What if Brochan was still upset about the cows? Worse, what if he regretted kissing her?

Brochan wondered if Cristy was sorry she'd kissed him. She stood near the fire with her eyes downcast. But it was hard to believe she hadn't felt the same world-shattering desire he had, the longing that didn't seem to be going away any time soon.

He wouldn't do anything about it, of course. As pleasurable as the kiss was, it had been impulsive and improper. It was dishonorable to seduce innocents.

Besides, he owed his loyalty to the mother of his sons. Didn't he?

Those sons flanked Cristy at the moment like knights standing guard, ready to defend their lady. The sight almost made him wish he could just forget about their disobedience. Almost.

"Ye've all had time to consider your actions," Brochan said with forced calm, closing the door behind him. "So tell me, which o' ye deserves the punishment for this?"

"I do, Da," Cambel volunteered. "I should have been watchin' o'er the lady so she wouldn't get hurt by the coos."

"Nay, 'twas my fault," said Colin. "'Twas my idea to reive Eufemie."

"Nonsense," Cristy said. "Ye're only wee lads. 'Twas my fault for takin' ye out to the coos without your Da's consent."

Brochan tried not to smile. He was actually very proud that his sons were willing to take the blame. It proved they were men of character.

And the fact that Cristy too was trying to protect them warmed his heart. He was glad he'd made the decision he had about her.

"And what do ye think your punishment should be?" he asked.

"Pickin' up coo pats?" said Colin with a sigh.

Cambel shuddered. "Cleanin' out the garderobe?"

Cristy glanced up and opened her mouth. No words came out. But he didn't think he'd be able to understand them anyway. Seeing her rosy lips again heated his blood and scattered his thoughts.

He cleared his throat. "I think ye all bear a wee bit o' the blame. So here's your punishment." He didn't tell them it was a task he'd intended for the lads all along. "The doocot is in need o' repair. The cracks need patchin' so the wind won't get through. So on the morrow, I want ye to mix up a batch o' clay, straw, and coo dung. Then ye'll have to daub it into the chinks to seal the walls from the weather."

Watching his sons try to hide their excitement over their punishment was amusing. They loved to be helpful, and repairing the dovecot was a chore that appealed to their sense of worth and independence. For Colin, especially eager to get his own flock of chickens, it was all the lad could do to keep from jumping up and down with glee.

Cristy, however, had a puzzled look on her face. "What news did the monk bring from my uncle?"

He hesitated. Of course, she expected she'd be going home before the morrow.

"M'lady doesn't have to go home, does she, Da?" Cambel folded his hands in supplication.

"She *has* to stay till the morrow," Colin declared, "for her punishment."

His sons apparently liked having her here almost as much as he did.

Cristy lifted her chin in challenge, but he could see her face had gone pale. "What did he say?"

Brochan straightened. He was now positive he was doing the right thing. "Your uncle agreed to return the five coos today to ransom ye," he lied.

He saw her jaw tense.

The lads wailed in protest.

He held up his hand to stop them. "But I told him I've changed my mind. I've decided five coos isn't nearly enough for a lady o' such quality."

"What?" Cristy was startled.

"I told him the ransom was now thirty coos."

Thirty? Thirty?

Cristy's jaw went slack. She couldn't believe Brochan had made such a demand. There was no way her uncle would pay such a price for her. That was over half of his herd.

She wanted to tell him so. She wanted to tell him his price was too dear.

But Brochan's words didn't escape her notice. He'd called her a lady of quality. That made her glow inside.

While the twins cheered and leaped for joy around her, she couldn't help but smile at Brochan. As hopeless as his demand was, it was immensely flattering.

The secret smile he gave her in return took her breath away. Suddenly she imagined she was back in the byre, pressing her fevered lips to his, brazenly exploring him with her hands, tasting the hot, wet length of his tongue, and longing for more.

Lust shadowed his eyes and flared his nostrils. He wanted her too.

Unfortunately, there were wee lads dancing about them at the moment and a dozen tasks he probably had to finish before the day was done.

If she helped, they'd go faster.

Then maybe she'd steal another kiss before she broke the news to him that her uncle was never going to send him thirty cows.

Beside her, Colin was counting on his fingers. "Thirty?" His eyes went round. "Are we goin' to get thirty coos, Da?" Before Brochan could answer, Colin took his brother by the shoulders and shook him with joy. "Cambel, we're goin' to get thirty more coos!"

Of course, the lads had overlooked the fact that they'd be trading Cristy for those cows. But her uncle wasn't going to send that many anyway, so it didn't matter.

"Now, lads," Brochan chided. "What is it Aesop said?"

Cambel said, "Slow and steady wins the race?"

"Well, aye," Brochan said, "but I'm thinkin' o' the *The Milkmaid and Her Pail.*"

"Och!" Colin cried. "Don't count your chickens ere they're hatched."

"That's the one," Brochan said.

Cristy had no idea what they were talking about, although not counting chickens until they're hatched seemed like a good suggestion.

"Do ye like Aesop's stories, m'lady?" Cambel asked.

"I don't know Aesop," she said.

"Da will tell ye some o' his stories," Colin confirmed. "Won't ye, Da?"

Cristy could see Brochan had a dozen things on his mind already. "Maybe later?" she suggested. "I fear your da is very busy today."

"I'll make ye a bargain," Brochan said. "Ye three come

help me clean out the pantry ere Mabel gets home, and I'll tell ye some of Aesop's stories while we work."

Unlike the much smaller buttery that Mabel used daily, the pantry was deep, dark, and cool. When Brochan brought down a candle stand so they could see better, the lads discovered an abundance of cobwebs and mouse droppings. It seemed that parts of the storeroom hadn't been touched by anything but vermin in years. Thick dust coated clay jars filled with unidentifiable substances that, when the corks were popped off, made the lads' noses wrinkle in displeasure. A few earthenware vessels had fallen, and shards of pottery were scattered on the floor. Mushrooms had sprouted on a few of the shelves, and the sack of barley slumped against the corner had long ago been chewed at the bottom, strewing grain everywhere.

Cristy would be surprised if anything was salvageable. Still, it had to be cleaned up to make room for the supplies Mabel was bringing home. So she pushed up the sleeves of her kirtle and grabbed the broom perched in the corner, determined to set the place to rights.

Brochan hauled in a great bucket of water, along with rags so they could clean as they went. He took the items off of the uppermost shelves and set them in the middle of the pantry. It was Colin's task to wipe away the dust and read the letters on the vessels to identify their contents. Cambel had the responsibility of peeking inside to determine if they were empty, rotten, or usable.

"Da, ye said ye'd tell us a story," Colin reminded him.

"Which story do ye want to hear?"

"The Lion and the Mouse!" Colin cried.

"Aye, *The Lion and the Mouse!*" Cambel echoed. "Ye'll like this one, m'lady."

While Cristy swept, Brochan told the story. "Once, a long while ago, a great lion was sleepin' in the woods..."

"Do ye know what a lion is, m'lady?" Cambel interrupted.

She smiled at his concerned expression. "Aye."

"As I said, a great lion was sleepin' in the woods. His enormous head was restin' on his paws, and he was snorin' as loud as...well, as loud as Rauf."

The lads giggled.

"Meanwhile, a timid wee mouse, payin' no heed to where she was goin', came upon the dozin' lion. In her hurry to get away from the dangerous beast, she accidentally ran straight across the lion's nose."

Cambel gasped dramatically, mostly for Cristy's benefit.

"O' course, the lion awoke at once, and, seein' the mouse, raised his big paw, intendin' to kill the wee beast that had disturbed his sleep."

The lads were enrapt and no longer toiling. Cristy, too, slowed her sweeping, transfixed both by the tale and by the sight of Brochan lifting heavy vessels off the top shelf, which made the impressive muscles of his back strain against the cloth of his leine.

"But then the mouse cried, 'Spare me, I beg ye!' 'Why should I spare ye?' said the lion. 'If ye spare me,' said the mouse, 'one day I shall repay ye for your kindness.'"

Cristy bit back a grin at the wee voice he'd given the mouse and the loud boom of the lion. No wonder his sons like the tales. Brochan was a gifted storyteller.

"Well, the lion didn't believe the mouse for one moment. After all, how could such a wee creature ever help a big and powerful lion? Nevertheless, he was amused by the minx of a mouse, and so he let her go."

Colin was squirming with anticipation. "Wait till ye find out what happens, m'lady."

"Many days later, the lion was chasin' after his supper in the same woods when he was caught in the tangle of a hunter's net. Unable to free himself from the ropes, no matter how much he twisted and turned, he let out a huge roar of anger."

"Do it, Da, do it!" Cambel cried.

Brochan gave Cristy a wink. Then he emitted a loud roar that left her heart in her throat, so savage was the sound.

The lads were giggling.

"Don't fret, m'lady," Cambel said. "'Tis only Da, not a real lion."

"Miss Moffat's not afraid o' lions, are ye, Miss Moffat?" Brochan asked.

If she was, she wasn't about to admit it. She lifted the broom. "Not while I have my trusty lion spear by my side."

The lads went wild with laughter then, which made her laugh in turn. She suddenly felt more giddy with joy—in a dark storeroom, holding a broom like a weapon, telling stories with two wee lads, admiring their father's hilarity and hindquarters—than she'd felt in years.

"Go on, Da," Colin said. "Tell m'lady what happens."

"Where was I? Och, aye, the roar. The mouse heard that roar and came at a run to find the lion strugglin' in the net. So, bein' a mouse o' her word, she nibbled and nibbled at the ropes until the grateful lion was free."

Colin clapped.

Brochan finished with, "The mouse said, 'Ye see? Even a wee creature like me can be o' help to a lion.'"

"Did ye like it, m'lady?" Cambel asked.

"Och, aye." Cristy could take the story to heart. For much of her life, she'd been made to feel like a mouse— wee, insignificant, useless.

"Now, lads, what's the moral o' the story?"

The lads recited, "Kindness is ne'er wasted."

Cristy smiled. It was a good moral.

"Tell us another, Da," Colin begged.

Brochan cocked an eye at them. "Ye finish those last few vessels, and then ye can start on the bottom shelves."

They hurried to do his bidding. Meanwhile, Cristy tied a damp rag around the handle end of the broom and swabbed away the cobwebs along the plaster ceiling.

"Will ye tell the story o' *The North Wind and the Sun,* Da?" Cambel asked when they started on the lower shelves.

Colin pouted. "But it doesn't have animals."

"'Tis a good story, though."

Colin shrugged. "I suppose."

"M'lady would like it."

"Would ye like it, m'lady?" Colin asked.

Cristy thought she'd happily listen to Brochan reciting the hours of the day, so pleasant was his voice. She nodded.

"Lady's choice 'tis," Brochan declared as he wiped down the top shelf. "One day, long ago, the North wind and the sun were bickerin', tryin' to decide which was the strongest. While they were arguin' in the road, a traveler happened to pass by."

Cambel gave his father a sly smile. "Did the traveler have a name?"

Brochan returned the grin. "Aye, as a matter o' fact, she did. Her name was Miss Moffat."

Cambel beamed. Apparently, it had been his plan all along to feature *her* in the story. She was enchanted.

Brochan continued. "The sun said to the wind, 'I know how we can settle this dispute. Whichever of us can strip the arisaid from that traveler—'"

"Miss Moffat," Cambel interjected with a giggle.

"Aye...'from that traveler, Miss Moffat, will be the strongest.' The North wind agreed and, all at once, blew a cold blast of air toward Miss Moffat."

"Do it, Da!" Cambel urged.

With a sheepish smile, Brochan pretended to blow out a long blast of air toward her. Caught up in the spirit of the play, Cristy feigned being blown backward by his North wind, which delighted the lads and made even Brochan laugh. So she continued to act out his story.

"Harder and harder the wind blew. One corner of the arisaid flew up, then the other. But Miss Moffat wrapped it close about her. The fiercer the wind blew, the tighter she held on to the arisaid. And finally the wind had to surrender."

Everyone was laughing at her antics. But it was Brochan's grin that made her melt.

He continued. "Then 'twas the sun's turn. The great yellow ball began to shine, very gently at first. Miss Moffat enjoyed the warmth after all the bitter cold o' the North wind. In fact, 'twas so pleasant that she unpinned her arisaid and loosened it a wee bit."

Cristy saw where the story was headed. And, feeling the way she did at the moment—lusty and daring—if she were alone with the laird, she might be tempted to actually remove her clothes, layer by layer. She settled for miming the actions, which seemed to satisfy the lads.

It also seemed to satisfy their father, whose eyes had taken on a shadowy cast.

"Warmer and warmer the sun burned," he said, "until Miss Moffat tossed back the hood o' her arisaid and mopped her brow."

She complied, wiping her forearm across her brow.

"The sun continued to blaze," he said, his voice a bit hoarser. "Cristy loosened the arisaid until it hung from her shoulders."

As she pretended to loosen her arisaid, Cristy watched Brochan. He might have been reciting a story, but his mind was clearly elsewhere. He was gazing at her with the same hunger she'd glimpsed in his eyes before, a hunger that sent a thrill through her.

"And then what, Da?" Colin urged.

Brochan licked his lips, staring at Cristy. "Then...then she...cast the arisaid away, because..."

From the level above came Mabel's voice. "Are ye down there, m'laird?"

Cristy clapped her hand to her bosom, as if she'd been caught disrobing.

"Aye!" His voice came out on a squeak. He cleared his throat. "Aye! In the pantry."

"We've brought the goods," she called down. "Can ye help Rauf unload them, m'laird?"

"I'll be right up."

"Da, ye have to finish the story," Colin said.

"Och, aye," he said in a rush. "So she tossed her arisaid aside, which meant the sun won. Now ye lads help Miss Moffat finish up the pantry while I unload the cart."

"But the moral, Da," Cambel reminded him.

"Right. What's the moral, lads?"

They replied, "Persuasion is better than force."

Cristy sighed as Brochan disappeared up the steps, her gaze lingering on his snug trews. Persuasion? It wouldn't take much to persuade her to kiss the irresistible laird again.

Brochan was glad of the heavy physical work, because it helped to take his mind off the enchanting lass in the pantry.

He was ashamed that he'd let lust take such control over him. For years, he'd kept it at bay, focusing on taking care of his sons, making a good life for his motherless lads. He felt he had to honor their mother's memory, and he'd never been tempted to look at another woman.

It was bad enough that he was drawn by Cristy's feminine lures—her lush black hair, her shining eyes, her succulent lips, her winsome figure. But now he was also attracted to her charming nature.

She was most remarkable, a lass of fascinating contrasts. Her spirit had been damaged in some ways, yet there was a willing playfulness about her. On the one hand, she seemed as innocent as his sons, yet on the other, she was worldly and wise beyond her years. She could be frail and fearful at times, fierce and frisky at others.

He liked her. It had been a long while since he'd said that about anyone. But he genuinely liked her.

And hours later, as they all sat together under the light of the comet—Cristy happily cradling both lads' sleepy heads in her lap—he wasn't sure "like" was a strong enough word.

CHAPTER 8

"**D**oes your da always punish ye like this, with chores?" Cristy asked the lads the next morn as they skipped hand-in-hand toward the dovecot. She still thought it was the most curious form of chastisement. Her uncle always backhanded her and her cousins when they did something wrong. But the lads seemed genuinely excited to do the work.

"We haven't done daub in a while," Colin said.

"Usually 'tis chamber pots," Cambel added.

"Does he never clout ye?" she asked.

The boys looked at her as if she were mad.

"Why would he clout us?" Cambel asked.

"That would be ungentlemanly," Colin said.

Cristy frowned. "But what's to keep ye from disobeyin' him again if ye're not afraid to be clouted?"

The lads looked at each other, pondering the question.

"'Twould make Da unhappy," Colin finally decided.

"Aye, and 'tis dishonorable," Cambel added.

"Da would never use force against us," Colin assured her.

"Aye, that's it!" Cambel said. "'Tis like the story about the North wind and the sun."

Together the lads said, "Persuasion is better than force."

Cristy lifted her brows. Was that true? Had Brochan *never* clouted his sons? Had he managed to raise these two wee gentleman with their kind manners and courteous speech without raising his hand to them?

She shook her head in wonder. Perhaps persuasion *was* better than force.

Daubing the dovecot might not have seemed much like punishment to Cristy, but it promised to be dirty work. So once inside the stone structure, she brought the back of her skirt between her legs to the front, looping it up to tuck it into her belt like the crofters did. There was no point in getting the hem any filthier than it already was.

"Ye'll have to show me how to make the daub," she said.

Colin and Cambel took pride in demonstrating their very precise recipe. They showed her exactly how many handfuls of straw, clay, and cow dung to use, though she insisted they employ a spade to measure out the cow dung. They mixed it all in a large wooden bucket, stirring it with a stick until it made a thick paste.

Then, using a few small spades, they began to daub the mixture into every cranny where the sunlight streamed through.

"Da says we can get chickens when the doocot is repaired," Cambel said.

"I can't wait to get chickens." Colin wiped his cheek, leaving a streak of daub there. "I'm goin' to be in charge o' collectin' the eggs every day."

"I'm goin' to be in charge o' the pigs when we get them," said Cambel.

"What are ye goin' to be in charge o', m'lady?" Colin asked.

"I…" she began awkwardly.

Cambel elbowed his brother. "She's goin' home, Colin. Remember? Da said when we get the thirty coos, she's goin' home."

Colin pursed his lips in a sad pout. "I don't want her to go home."

"But ye like coos, Colin."

Colin's chin trembled. "I don't like coos as much as I like m'lady."

Cristy felt her heart cave in at his words. No one had ever said such a sweet thing. She bit her lip to keep from crying.

Cambel consoled his brother. "But she promised she'd come and visit us, right, m'lady?"

She didn't trust herself to speak, so she just nodded, hoping she could keep her promise. She knew it was only a matter of time before the ransom was paid. It wouldn't be thirty cows. That was a preposterous number. But her uncle would at least return Macintosh's own cattle. And then she'd have to leave. But it wouldn't surprise her if Douglas Moffat forbid her from venturing to the Macintosh holding after that.

It took over an hour to use up the first bucket of daub, though a good portion of it seemed to have found its way onto their clothing. While the lads were mixing another batch, Cristy surveyed the dovecot. The interior was dimmer, now that they'd filled in the lower crevices. She decided they should have the door open for light.

As she swung the door wide, something fluttered out of the path. It looked like a scrap of crumpled parchment. She bent down to pick it up. As she did, she noticed another piece. She compared them. They fit together. Someone or something had torn the parchment in half. There was scrawling on one side, but she couldn't read it.

An inexplicable tingling suddenly traversed the back of her neck, as if she'd backed into a spider's web.

"Lads," she said, wandering back into the dovecot, "do ye know what this is?"

They glanced at the two pieces.

"Parchment?" Colin guessed.

"Can ye tell me what it says?" she asked.

They frowned in concentration as they bowed their heads over the two scraps, deciphering the letters.

"Keep her," Colin said. "It says 'keep her.' But I can't read *this* word."

"'Tis too messy," Cambel said.

She stared closer at it. She'd seen that scrawl before. "Moffat."

Cambel shrugged. "Maybe."

Keep her. Moffat.

The letters blurred as she continued to stare at them.

Suddenly she felt dizzy. Then sick. Then numb. Her blood congealed in her veins. And her heart seemed to shrivel in her chest.

Cristy's worst fears were confirmed. She didn't belong. She wasn't wanted.

"What does it mean?" Colin wanted to know.

How could she answer him?

What it meant was that she was alone in the world. That her own uncle didn't care about her. That nobody cared about her.

"Are ye all right, m'lady?" Cambel asked, resting a dirty but concerned hand on her skirt.

She looked blankly down at him.

But that wasn't right. Someone *did* care about her. These two lads cared about her. They thought she was bonnie...and better than cows.

And then, as she let the pieces of parchment flutter to the ground, she realized someone else cared even more about her.

Brochan.

This note was for him. He must have read it. And he must have torn it in half.

He'd lied to her.

There had been no fierce negotiations. Her uncle hadn't been willing to trade for her at all. And Brochan hadn't demanded thirty cows for her return. He'd only said that because he knew there was going to be no return.

He'd made all of that up to keep her from being hurt. He'd tried to protect her feelings.

Her deflated heart slowly filled again—with wonder, with warmth, with joy.

The Macintoshes cared about her. The lads called her "m'lady" and snuggled with her at night and laughed at her playacting. Brochan treated her like a guest, guarded her heart from pain, and kissed her with tenderness.

She dared to wonder if she might make a home here, if she might be able to find a place in their kind and loving household.

She would do whatever it took to earn their trust and be deserving of their love. She'd empty the chamber pots, scrub the garderobe, and pick up coo pats every day if it meant she could be part of their clan.

With a trembling smile, she placed a hand atop Cambel's sweet head. "I'm all right. Everythin' is goin' to be all right."

Her spirits renewed, she straightened and looked around the dovecot. There were still a lot of gaps to fill, but the sooner she finished, the sooner her darling wee companions would be able to get their beloved chickens.

Her ambitious plans were curtailed when the lads started quibbling.

"Don't!" Colin snapped at Cambel, ducking his head away.

"I'm just tryin' to get the daub off your face," Cambel argued.

"Nay, ye're not! Ye're puttin' more on!"

"Lads," Cristy chided.

They ignored her.

In perceived retaliation, Colin dipped his finger in the daub and smudged it on Cambel's cheek.

Cambel's eyes went wide in disbelief. "Colin! For shame!"

Colin giggled.

Cambel dipped his whole hand in the bucket then and put a handprint in the middle of Colin's white leine.

Colin's jaw dropped.

"Lads!" Cristy scolded, planting her hands on her hips.

In return, Colin grabbed a fistful of daub and smeared it across Cambel's leine.

Cambel gasped.

Then began the melee. The lads started reaching into the bucket and firing sticky handfuls at each other as if engaged in a deadly battle. Soon, brown splats covered their hair and clothing and stuck to the walls of the byre.

"Lads!" she shouted.

Then one of the twins—she wasn't sure which one—happened by chance to fire a daub missile straight at her. It caught her on the forehead.

All three of them froze in horror as the daub began dripping down her nose.

Cristy didn't know what got into her. She acted on instinct. With a vexed growl, she reached both her hands into the bucket and smacked the mischievous lads in the face with daub.

Unfortunately, that only escalated the fight. Colin

accused Cambel of attacking Cristy, and Cambel accused Colin. They began pelting each other again. And Cristy found herself elbow-deep in the battle.

Not long after that the giggles started.

Brochan smiled as he strode down the brae toward the dovecot. His penitents didn't sound very penitent. He could hear laughter coming from inside. The sound of his sons laughing always lifted his spirits. But hearing Cristy's giggles mingled with theirs was like listening to merry music.

He wondered what had made them so full of cheer.

The door was open, so he poked his head inside. "What's goin' on, my wee merrymak-?"

His question was cut short by the smack of something against his chest. Something wet and brown and sticky.

"What the...?"

Frozen before him, looking as filthy as pigs and guilty as sin, were his sons and his hostage. It didn't escape his notice that Miss Moffat's skirts were hitched up like a crofter's, leaving her mouthwatering legs indecently bare, albeit coated with nasty-looking mire. Indeed, if he weren't so appalled by the mess, he might have been aroused.

He lifted his fingers to his chest and drew them back with a scowl. Daub. One of the three miscreants before him had thrown daub at him.

"I can explain," Cristy said. At least he *thought* it was Cristy. It was hard to tell under all that muck.

"I'm sorry, Da."

"We're sorry, Da."

For the first time in his life, Brochan wasn't sure which twin was which. Their faces were covered in mire, and straw stuck out at all angles from their hair.

He shook his head in disbelief. It looked as if they'd been having some sort of full-scale daub war.

Then Cristy snickered.

The lads covered their mouths, stifling giggles.

Brochan glowered at them from the doorway, his arms crossed sternly over his chest—just below the splash of daub.

But the mischief-makers couldn't contain their laughter, and soon the rafters of the dovecot were ringing with the sound of unfettered glee.

Brochan narrowed his gaze and gave them a dire warning. "If ye think I'm goin' to let ye get away with this, ye're mistaken."

He then proceeded to do what any wise laird would do to maintain the upper hand and establish his dominance. He joined in the battle and defeated them all soundly.

When they ran out of munitions, they collapsed in a laughing heap on the floor of the dovecot. Daub not only caked their clothing and stained their skin. Muddy splats also decked the walls and littered the floor.

But it was worth it to hear their laughter. For the first time in too many days, now that he had an extra helping hand, Brochan felt he could spare a few moments for frivolity.

Of course, the mess had to be cleaned up. And the lads

needed to be scrubbed from head to toe before he'd let them into the tower house.

"Ye know what this means, lads," he said.

One of them sighed. "Since we were wicked, do we have to clean out the garderobe?"

"Ye already *smell* like a garderobe," he told them. "But nay. I think we need to make a trip to the loch to get the stink off."

The lads cheered. They hated their weekly bath in a tub, but in summer, they were always keen to take a dip in a loch.

Before Brochan could exercise prudence, the lads extended an invitation to Cristy.

"Ye come with us, m'lady! Ye'll love the loch!"

"Aye, and ye can get the stink off ye too!"

Cristy hesitated. "I'm not sure your da—"

"Please, m'lady," one of the twins begged. "I want to show ye the frogs."

"And I can swim. Ye have to see how I can swim."

After that, despite Brochan's qualms about inviting a lass to bathe with them, he knew she could hardly refuse.

"Fine. I'll come."

At first, frolicking in the loch was fairly harmless. Since their clothing was coated with muck, the lads waded in, fully dressed, to rinse it out of their trews and leines.

But the lads were unaccustomed to swimming in their clothes. So they very quickly and unabashedly peeled off their soaking garments, tossing them atop a boulder at the water's edge, and returned to swimming and splashing about like a pair of naked kelpies.

The lads took turns showing Cristy how well they could swim, and she praised their efforts. Of course, though she could wade into the water, she dared not go too deep. Her drenched wool skirts would pull her under. So she stood waist-deep in the loch, washing her face and loosening her braid in the sunshine.

While she watched the twins, Brochan watched her.

It seemed like Cristy had blossomed in the last few days. That first night, her face had been full of fear and hate and anger. But now she was radiant. Her eyes were joyful. Her head was held high. Her smile was wide and open. She was truly beautiful—in body and in spirit.

He wanted to keep her...forever.

Then he was struck with a bolt of guilt. That was the promise he'd given his wife.

Besides, it was a foolish wish. Cristy didn't belong to him. Even if her kin refused to negotiate for her return, he couldn't help but believe that, deep in her heart, she longed to go home.

The kiss they'd shared had been an accident, something fleeting and meaningless. The last thing a carefree young lass like Cristy wanted was to be tied to a man with two wee sons, two old servants, and a holding he could barely manage.

So then what was he going to do with her? He'd delayed her leaving, both to salvage her feelings and because he selfishly wasn't ready to part with her yet. But he couldn't keep up the pretense of holding her hostage. At some point, he had to let her go.

He knew that. So why did it agonize him so much to think about it?

Cristy smiled at the lads, clapping her hands in approval as they showed her the pebbles they'd collected from the loch bottom.

His chest ached as he thought of no longer having her in his life. True, he'd only known her a few days. But in that short time, she'd already become fast friends with his sons, and she'd already made a place for herself in his heart.

It wasn't the place his wife occupied. No one would ever have that place.

But he'd grown undeniably fond of Cristy. And since he cared about her, as much as it pained him, he had to tell her the truth. It was the right thing to do.

With a resigned sigh, he called out, "Lads, are ye good and clean?"

They groaned in protest. If it were up to them, they'd swim in the loch all day.

"Ye need to get back to the tower and give Mabel your wet clothes."

"But, Da…"

"Please, Da, we want to stay."

"If ye stay, ye won't get your chores done. And if ye don't get your chores done, ye won't get to see the comet tonight."

"I don't mind," Colin said. "I've seen the comet."

"Me neither," said Cambel. "I'd rather stay here and swim."

Brochan could honestly say he didn't blame them. Cristy's company was much more engaging than a star hanging silently in the sky. But he needed some time alone with her.

Remembering that persuasion was better than force, he said, "I'll make a bargain with ye. If ye get into dry clothes and finish your chores, I'll tell ye another story tonight."

"*The Oak and the Reed?*" Cambel asked.

"Nay, *The Tortoise and the Hare!*" Colin cried.

"Ye always get *The Tortoise and the Hare,*" Cambel complained.

"Whoever gets to the tower first can pick the tale," Brochan decided.

The lads sprang out of the loch, dripping, grabbed their clothes, and skipped toward the tower house, naked as newborns.

"Don't go near the cattle!" he yelled after them.

"We won't!" they called back.

He watched them scamper away for as long as he could, loath to confront Cristy with the painful news he had. When he could delay no more, he turned back...and froze.

Her clothes were in a pile at the loch's edge. Afloat in the water, letting the current lap at her bare shoulders, was beautiful Cristy, wearing naught but a smile.

He didn't know whether to be pleased or horrified. Fairly quickly, his body made up his mind for him. Within his trews, he felt a swelling as he continued to gaze at her and imagined what lay hidden beneath the waves.

"Are ye goin' to stand there all day?" she teased.

He gulped. "Maybe."

She obviously didn't know the power of her own beauty. There was no way to have a serious discussion with the lass while she was naked and so damned tempting.

"Why?" she asked sincerely. "Don't ye know how to swim?"

"O' course I know how to swim."

"Then come join me," she cooed, playfully twirling in the water.

She bobbed up briefly enough for him to catch a glimpse of a pair of lovely, pale breasts with dark points just beneath the surface. His mouth went dry.

"Ye aren't afraid o' me, are ye?" she teased.

He scoffed, though it came out as more of a croak.

But aye, he was afraid of her. She made him think of mad things, like forgetting his marriage vows, kissing her again, and holding her hostage forever.

Bloody hell.

"Ye're not afraid I'm a kelpie, here to lure ye to your doom?" she said with a laugh.

That was exactly what he was afraid of.

But he couldn't very well turn down her perfectly innocent invitation. She didn't mean anything by it. And he wasn't a coward.

With a sigh of defeat and determined to keep things as casual as possible, he began stripping off his clothes.

CHAPTER 9

Cristy's invitation was anything but innocent.

She wasn't unaware of the effect she was having on Brochan. She wanted him to kiss her again. And she knew that men, like cattle, could be more easily moved when they were guided along. Just as he'd said, persuasion was better than force. So she intended to persuade him.

What she didn't expect was the effect Brochan would have on *her* once he started undressing.

When he whipped off his leine, her breath caught in lusty surprise. His bare chest was taut with muscle, his stomach ridged, narrowing to a trim waist. His shoulders were broad, and his arms were massive. No wonder he'd been able to pack her off to the tower house with such ease that first night.

She swallowed hard as he hastily untied and stepped out of his trews to reveal powerful thighs and lean calves. For a startling instant, she imagined those legs tangled in bedsheets with hers, and a sudden twinge of need pulsed at her core.

Then he began untying the linen braies beneath. Anticipation sent a curious heat through her, humming around her head and diving deep between her legs.

All at once, his braies were undone. In one swift motion, he cast them off and headed toward the water.

A single fleeting glimpse of him sent a bolt of lust arcing through her. He was magnificent—bold and confident and strong—and something about the pure male energy of his body called to her womanly yearning. Though she'd never lain with a man before, she craved Brochan, longed to feel him beside her and, aye, within her.

That burning desire was instantly doused when Brochan entered the loch with a great surge of water that went over her head.

She came up choking and sputtering.

"Och, my apologies," he said, though there was a betraying twinkle in his eye. "Are ye all right?"

She answered him with a punitive splash of water. "Ye did that on purpose."

"Who, me?"

"Ye big..." She stopped to cough out the last of the water. "Whale."

He laughed. "Did ye just call me a whale?"

"I did." She stifled her own laughter.

"Well, if ye didn't swim like a cat..." he teased.

Her mouth gaped open, and she almost got a mouthful of water again.

"See?" he said.

She narrowed her eyes in feigned fury. She didn't swim like a cat. Using both hands, she started splashing him relentlessly, keeping up a barrage of water.

At first he held up his arms in defense. Then he sank beneath the surface.

Suddenly something pinched her toe, and even though she knew it was him, she yanked her foot back with a shriek. He grabbed her other toe, and she yelped, kicking it out of his grasp.

Then they collided, and she clearly felt his leg brush the side of her hip.

Startled, she thrashed around, and her hand grazed his chest.

When he broke the surface of the water, he was facing her.

Though there was still a residual smile on his face, his eyes sobered as he realized how close they were.

Panicked, Cristy raised her hands with the intent of splashing him away again. He caught her wrists to stop her.

And then the levity of the moment was gone. Time seemed to stand still.

This close, she could see the veil of desire muting his bright green eyes and the subtle flare of his nostrils as he gazed back at her. Water dripped with slow sensuality down the stubbled plane of his face and onto the wide expanse of his chest. But it was his mouth—his beautiful, delicious mouth—that truly tempted her.

When his eyes lowered to her lips, she parted them with a gasp. The craving in his gaze fueled her own. As they drew closer and closer, the water lapped sensuously at their bodies. And as they stared at each other, a powerful current snapped between them, shocking her to life.

She wanted him—all of him.

She let her eyes drift closed and tipped her head back, waiting breathlessly for his kiss.

He didn't disappoint. When he released her wrists, it was only to delve his hands into her hair and bring her near. His lips claimed hers with barely contained ferocity, sending an erotic shiver up her spine.

She moaned against his mouth and snaked her arms around his neck, reeling at the divine sensation of flesh on flesh as she melted against his muscular chest. Their tongues swirled together in the language of lust. And when she brazenly thrust her hips against his, she felt his bold arousal making its own silent demand.

When his lips left hers to nuzzle her cheek, she tipped back her head, and he rained kisses along her neck. He licked the sensitive spot beneath her ear, and she quivered, digging her fingers into his back.

Beyond reason, beyond care, her focus was drawn to the fiery yearning between her legs. Pure instinct made her grind against him, seeking to alleviate the burn.

He groaned and shuddered.

Buoyed by the water and using his shoulders for leverage, she lifted herself, entwining her legs around his waist. The warm skin of his torso felt heavenly against her inner thighs. But there was still an intense ache at her center, an emptiness longing to be filled.

In some remote corner of her mind, Cristy was mortified by her own wanton urges. But this new woman she'd become was beyond thought. Driven by passion, she followed her instincts without shame. And those instincts were telling her to join with him. Now.

Brochan had never wanted anything as much as he wanted Cristy at this moment. Maybe it was because of long abstinence, but he feared in another moment he'd explode. Every inch of him was aroused. Every nerve was on fire.

He was fast losing control. And if he lost control, he might do something foolish. Like consummate his desire with a woman who was not his wife, a woman who was probably a virgin.

So with every ounce of fortitude he could muster, he pushed down his carnal cravings and resisted her seduction, not because it was what he wanted, but because it was the right thing to do.

He eased her luscious legs from around his waist and loosed her arms from his neck, setting her away from him.

He thought she'd be grateful. After all, he was doing the responsible thing. He was taking charge of their indiscretion and guarding her maidenhood.

He couldn't have been more wrong. Instead of relief, her face was etched with betrayal and disappointment. She assumed he was rejecting her.

How could he explain that he was releasing her, not

because he didn't desire her—bloody hell, how he desired her—but out of honor, duty, propriety, and for her own welfare?

Naught was going to smooth the crease of disillusionment from her brow—at least naught he could *say*.

But he could *do* something to reassure her, something to convince her that she was worthy and desirable and seductive and irresistible.

Ignoring his own raging lust, he engaged her again, kissing her pouting lips and caressing her ear between his thumb and finger. She succumbed almost at once, closing her eyes and leaning into his embrace.

He let his fingertips trace the throbbing vein along her throat. He grazed her bosom with the back of his knuckles. Her breath was ragged against his mouth as she arched her back, urging him to venture farther.

Inch by inch, he complied. Despite his unrequited arousal, he relished her increasing desire. At last, he brushed the stiffened points of her nipples, eliciting a gasp of wonder from her. He kissed her again as he cupped her lovely breasts, weighing them in his palms, stroking her wet, velvety skin.

Then he made a trail of kisses down her throat, nibbling at the place beneath her ear until she squirmed with pleasure. When his mouth drifted down to her bosom, she held her breath in anticipation.

Her hands tangled in his hair as he locked his lips upon her breast, feeding upon her ecstasy.

While she reveled in that delight, he moved his hand

lower, into the water, sweeping over her ribs, venturing across her stomach, and playing in the soft curls that guarded her maidenhood.

All the while, her sounds of sensuous distress were driving him mad. With every fiber of his being, he longed to lie with her.

So he did the next best thing.

Lifting her in his arms, he conveyed her across the water to the shore. There he lay her down in the shallows where the water was warmer and he could rightfully worship her beautiful body. Answering the question in her eyes, he stretched out beside her, holding her hand in his and letting his free hand follow a sinuous path toward the target of her need.

She flushed with amazed pleasure as his fingers slipped through her womanly curls and between her swollen nether lips.

His smile was strained as his body responded with painful force to what he was touching, imagining all too well how those soft folds would feel around his rigid staff.

Cristy felt like she was adrift in deep, uncharted waters. But though the feelings were dangerously new to her, she felt safe in Brochan's arms. Lying back on the soft bank in the shallow waves, she was soothed by the lap of the water even as she was aroused by the lovely movement of his fingers upon her most secret place.

She throbbed with need, and what he did was

intensifying that yearning. She locked her hands behind his neck, squeezing her eyes shut as her body strained and swelled until she thought she would burst. Sharper and sharper her desire grew, centering at the spot where he stroked her with nimble skill. At last, able to endure no more, she stiffened, and the breath stilled in her lungs.

For what seemed an eternity, she hung in silent weightlessness, like an angel soaring high above the earth. And then, all at once, she plunged downward at breakneck speed, clinging to Brochan for dear life as she thrashed beneath him in the throes of ecstasy.

When she finally recovered, gasping for breath and glowing with relief, she opened her eyes to slits and peered up at Brochan.

There was a look of feral hunger on his face. His jaw was clamped shut. His brow was deeply creased. Like a bull ready to charge, his nostrils flared and his eyes darkened.

She wouldn't have believed it possible, but his expression sent her passions rising again. She suddenly longed to quell his craving the way he had hers. And though she knew it was improper to think such things, she wondered...if he could bring her to such a lovely anguish with only the light touch of his fingers, what could the rest of him do?

She had to act quickly, before too much reflection could make a coward of her. Having no idea what she was doing, she acted on impulse. While he was yet fully aroused, she positioned herself to accept him. Then she wrapped her legs around his hips and arched upward.

His groan startled her, but not as much as the sharp slice of pain inside her, followed by an impossible fullness. She gasped and winced. Then she looked askance at him.

His face was troubled. Had she hurt him? Had she damaged herself?

"Och, lass, I'm sorry," he wheezed out, as if it were his fault. "Are ye hurt?"

She furrowed her brow. "Did I do somethin' wrong?"

"Nay, but..." He squeezed his eyes closed and moaned again. She felt him pulse inside her.

"Did I hurt ye?" she whispered.

He broke out instantly into the most curious grin— part amusement, part disbelief, part regret. Then he shook his head. "'Tis the furthest thing from hurt," he assured her.

She gulped with relief.

"But Cristy," he breathed. "I didn't mean for ye to get hurt."

She gave him a small, reassuring smile. Already the pain was fading.

"If ye'll let me," he promised, "I can make it better for ye."

She nodded.

He did make it better. He caressed her breasts with a delicate hand and breathed gentle encouragements into her ear as he slowly moved inside her. With painstaking patience and exquisite languor, he pushed against her until his breath grew uneven. Gradually, her pain diminished into desire. Soon, she was answering the dance, moving her hips and digging eager heels into his buttocks.

Again, her senses spiraled upward. And she could tell, peering at him through her lashes, that he was experiencing the same unbridled yearning. They suffered together, gasping for breath, moaning in glorious torment, until they could climb no more.

With a great primitive cry that called to Cristy and shook her to the core, Brochan erupted, spilling his seed into her with all the force of his passion. She joined him on that sensual skyward journey, and they rocked together until they fell softly back to earth.

As Cristy lay spent on the shore, she couldn't help but smile. She'd never been more content. The sun shone gently upon them. The loch plashed in playful waves around them. His hot breath rasped against her ear. His skin was warm and slippery against hers. And joined as they were, she felt as if she'd become one with him, as if they would never again be apart, as if she finally belonged.

Silently, Brochan cursed his carelessness. How could he have done something so dishonorable? He'd let lust get the better of him.

Aye, he'd never felt such pure elation, trysting with Cristy. He was ashamed to admit he'd never shared such depths of passion, even with his wife. But it wasn't right. He'd taken her virginity, for God's sake. Worse, he hadn't even taken precautions to make sure he wouldn't give her a child.

He would never believe it was Cristy's fault, even if she had impaled herself upon him. He knew better. He alone was responsible. He should never have put her in such a risky situation.

When he raised his head to gaze into Cristy's eyes—her bliss-filled, shining eyes—he was filled with remorse.

The men in her life had abused her. Her uncle beat her. Her cousins treated her with scorn. He couldn't join the ranks of those who inflicted damage upon Cristy. He couldn't deflower the innocent lass and turn her out into the world, a victim of his recklessness.

He had to make things right. He had to do the honorable thing.

And if his heart quickened—imagining her in his arms every night, waking to her beautiful face every morn—he pushed those thoughts away. He told himself it was not a matter of replacing his wife. He was only taking responsibility for his actions.

"That was...magnificent," Cristy sighed, gazing up at him with lust-languid eyes.

He quirked up the corner of his mouth, but there was a guilty lump in his throat now that wouldn't let him speak.

He'd made a grave mistake. And decency required he pay for it.

He convinced himself he would have done the same for any lass he'd compromised. It made no difference that Cristy had delectable brown eyes, honey lips, and a body that made him feel alive. It didn't matter that she had a wicked sense of humor and a delightful laugh, that she was beloved by his sons and his servants, that she felt like a fresh summer breeze blowing into his world.

No one would ever usurp his first wife's place in his heart. He'd sworn to love her forever, and he was a man of his word.

As he tucked a hand behind Cristy's head, first to give her a fond kiss and then to lift her out of the water, he made a silent vow. When they got back to the tower house, he'd make things right. Though it meant yet another person to be responsible for, he would accept the burden of his sin and ask her to be his wife.

By the time they climbed the motte, hand-in-hand, Cristy's hair was almost dry. Her kirtle was still damp, but she felt so warm and glowing inside that she hardly noticed.

She wondered if she looked different. She *felt* different—transformed, just as Brighde had predicted. Certainly if she didn't stop smiling, Mabel would know at once what they'd done.

Halfway to the door, Brochan stopped. He clasped her hand between both of his and cleared his throat.

Cristy's heart leaped. This was it. He was going to ask her to marry him.

He'd tell her that he'd fallen in love with her, that he didn't think he could live without her, that he wanted to give her children, and that he promised to love her forever if she would only agree to be his wife.

She waited breathlessly.

"I've been givin' it some thought," he said, his face very serious as he stared at the ground between them. "What will happen if your uncle doesn't send the thirty cows? Would that be so terrible? From what ye say, there's not much for ye to go back to as his ward. My lads are in sore need of motherin'. And there's too much work here for Mabel to do on her own. What I'm askin' is if ye think ye might be willin' to stay here at the tower house."

Cristy blinked in displeased surprise. That wasn't the love-struck confession she'd imagined at all. "Stay? What do ye mean, stay? Ye mean, as your servant?"

"Och, nay," he said glancing up at her and then returning to scowl at the ground. "I wonder if ye might be willin' to...ye know, to live with me as husband and wife."

Cristy was stunned. Was that it? Was that his romantic proposal?

What was wrong with him?

Was it possible she'd misjudged him?

"Do ye love me?" she asked.

He gulped and took too long to answer. "I could *grow* to love ye."

She felt his honesty like a dagger in her chest. As much as she wanted to accept his offer and become Lady Cristy Macintosh, she couldn't wed a man whose heart didn't belong to her.

So she withdrew her hand. "Then nay."

"Nay!" His amazement was clear in his eyes. "What do ye mean, nay?"

"I won't marry ye."

"But we trys-..." He lowered his voice, in case the

servants or his sons were about. "We trysted together. I took your virginity."

His words only made things worse. Not only did he apparently not love her. He was only asking her to marry him out of guilt and duty.

"Ye didn't take my virginity," she corrected. "I gave it to ye." Her own admission upset her. How could she have given her virginity to a man who didn't even love her?

"Ye won't marry me?" He seemed utterly astounded. "But why?"

If he was too blind to see that she was not interested in merely a marriage of convenience, she wasn't going to tell him. She gave him an irritating shrug.

"But what if ye're...with child?" he whispered.

She suppressed a gasp. She hadn't considered that. Was that the real reason he was proposing—because he thought he had to rescue her from shame?

"If I'm with child," she said with flippancy she didn't feel, "then I'll go back where I belong and raise it myself." Her voice caught on the word "belong," for she knew she didn't belong in the Moffat household—not really.

The shock in his face rapidly turned to frustration and then menace. "I...I forbid it. If ye're with child, 'twill belong to me." He crossed his arms over his chest, as if his word was final.

Her jaw dropped. Their conversation had taken a nasty turn. "Ye can't take away my child."

"*My* child," he said with an imperious arch of his brow. "And I won't allow a child o' mine to be raised in your savage uncle's household."

She narrowed her eyes at him. She didn't want a child raised in her uncle's household either. But she wasn't about to let cocky Brochan Macintosh order her about as if he owned her now, just because they'd trysted once. "Ye won't have any choice. Once ye get your coos, I'll be free to go."

It was a foolish statement. She knew about the missive. Her uncle wasn't going to ransom her.

But rather than admit her threat was empty, she wheeled and stomped off toward the door.

Just before she slammed it behind her, Brochan got in the last word. "He's not goin' to send any coos! He doesn't want ye back!"

CHAPTER 10

Brochan grimaced, regretting his words the instant they left his lips. He hadn't meant to blurt that out. The truth was he'd panicked. And it was the only thing he could think of that might keep her from leaving him.

And then reality hit him. He was terrified of losing her.

But why?

When he realized the answer, he staggered back a step, shaken.

God help him, he *was* in love with her. He was in love with Cristy Moffat.

As impetuous and improbable as it was, he'd fallen in love with the outlaw lass who'd reived his coos.

But then who wouldn't love her? She was sweet and spirited, playful and passionate, lovely and loving, all any man could want.

Why then was it so hard to admit that?

Why had he given her every reason for marrying him but that one?

Wrestling with his conscience, he turned, slogging back down the motte and toward the byre.

It was his wife, he realized.

He still felt he had to be faithful to his wife.

Of course, he knew that was naïve. His wife wasn't coming back. She'd left this world.

Besides, as Mabel ceaselessly reminded him, she wouldn't have wanted Brochan to be lonely. She would have wanted him to wed again.

That might be true, he thought, but would she have wanted him to *love* again?

He entered the dim byre, noting that the milk buckets were empty. The twins hadn't done the second milking yet. He'd send them out after dinner. He studied the sagging thatch overhead that would need to be repaired before winter. And he wondered what his wife would have thought of Cristy.

He closed his eyes and tried to conjure up his wife's image. But it was difficult. And that troubled him. Her face should be etched indelibly in his conscience. And yet the longer she was gone, the more indistinct her features became. Soon, he feared, she'd be but a wisp of a memory.

Yet maybe that was as it should be. Maybe life was kind that way, gently smoothing away the edges of a person's face, like water polishing rock, until recalling her was less painful.

Five years she'd been gone. Five years he'd been without a woman. And though his sons had kept him from despair, giving him something to live for, they hadn't brought him the companionship he craved, the love of an adoring wife.

He leaned back against the byre wall.

He decided his wife would have liked Cristy. After all, her sons did. And Mabel and Rauf, who had been his wife's most trusted servants, liked her as well.

Maybe it was time.

Maybe his wife would forgive him for loving another.

As he pushed away from the wall and ambled back up to the tower house by the fading light of day, he felt at peace for the first time in years.

Then he remembered the strange tavern wench and her prophecy.

Maybe Brighde had been right.

Maybe it was time to change his stars.

As he entered the hall, however, he first had to attend to his clamoring sons, who rushed up the instant he arrived.

"Da! I won! I won!" Cambel said.

"Aye," said Colin, "Cambel got here first."

"Colin would have won if he hadn't tripped o'er a dry coo pat."

"I did trip o'er a coo pat," Colin admitted with a shrug.

"But we talked it o'er," Cambel said.

"And we both want the same story," Colin said.

Brochan put a hand on each of their heads. But his attention drifted to the beautiful lass standing by the fire to dry her skirts. He could hardly believe she was the same eager and passionate woman he'd made love to at the loch's edge. She was staring silently into the flames. Her expression was distant and elusive.

Colin tugged on his leine. "Don't ye want to know what story we chose?"

"Aye," he said. "What story?"

They answered together. *"The Mice in Council."*

Brochan nodded his approval, but his mind was still on Cristy. He had to apologize to her. He should never have said such a hurtful thing. And somehow he had to convince her to stay. Most of all, he had to find a way to make her care for him the way he cared for her.

But just then Mabel announced dinner. Soon he became distracted by salmon pottage and bannocks, the babbling of his lads, and the servants' report of the day.

Cristy sat quietly between the twins, stirring her pottage, as if naught was wrong.

She wasn't hungry. Indeed, she didn't want to sit here at all. Part of her wanted to retreat somewhere to lick her wounds after Brochan's cruel reminder that her uncle didn't want her back. And part of her wanted to seize the stubborn laird by the front of his leine and demand that he admit to loving her.

She didn't dare do either. To leave would invite too many questions. Already, Mabel was eyeing her with suspicion because of her quiet mood. And Cristy didn't wish to upset the twins. So she only picked at her bannock and stared at her pottage while dinner continued around her.

"Da, can ye tell us the story now?" Cambel asked.

"Aye, Da, tell us." Colin tugged on Cristy's sleeve, and she looked askance at him. "Have ye heard *The Mice in Council* before, m'lady?"

She shook her head.

Cambel told her, "'Tis all about bravery."

"Don't spoil it, Cambel," said Colin.

"I won't."

"Because 'twill ruin the surprise."

"I know."

"Hush, lads," Mabel chided. "Let your da tell the tale."

Brochan took a drink of ale, then cleared his throat and began. "Once there was a great family o' mice that lived in the shadow of a very wicked cat."

Cristy tore off a chunk of bannock and dipped it into her pottage. She could tell by Brochan's voice that he wasn't in a storytelling mood. No doubt the disgruntled laird was unaccustomed to having his wedding proposals refused.

"Now this cat had a powerful cravin' for mouse meat. It seemed that every time a mouse crept out of its wee home, she was ready to spring out and snap it up in her claws."

"Da," Colin interjected, "do ye think we could get a cat?"

"Colin, don't interrupt," Cambel chided.

"I'm just wonderin'."

"A cat?" Brochan considered. "I suppose, as long as ye look after it and keep it out o' the doocot."

Colin cheered.

"Now where was I?" Brochan asked.

Cambel said, "Snappin' up mice in her claws."

"Aye. 'Twas so bad, all the mice were afraid to leave their homes. They decided to have a council…"

"A mice council," Colin gushed, as if the idea pleased him immensely. Cristy wondered if his opinion would change when his new cat started gifting him with dead mice.

"In that mice council," Brochan said, "they discussed the matter. One mouse suggested they kill the cat. But most o' the mice disapproved o' the idea. The cat, after all, couldn't help her nature. Another mouse declared they should have watch-mice set up at points along the wall to report when the cat was on the prowl. But then the youngest mouse—"

"Did the youngest mouse have a name?" Cambel wanted to know.

"A name? I suppose so. What do ye think 'twas?"

"Morris," Cambel decided.

"Right. His name was Morris the Mouse. So wee Morris stood up bravely before the others and said, 'I have a plan.' The older mice scoffed at him, for he was young and inexperienced in the ways o' cats. But they let him speak anyway. He said, 'Why don't we hang a bell around the cat's neck? That way, whene'er we hear the bell ringin', we'll know the cat is nigh.'"

It actually *was* a good idea. In fact, if Colin got his cat, Cristy would have to give him a bell to put around its neck.

Then she remembered…she might not be here when he got his cat.

The thought saddened her. She truly wished to stay—to watch the lads grow up, to help take care of the tower house, to look after the hardworking laird of Macintosh. But Cristy had lived long enough with men who didn't care for her. When she married, it would be to a man who loved her with all his heart.

"At first," Brochan continued with the story, "none o' the mice said a thing. Then, one by one, they saw the genius o' the idea and started exclaimin', 'Tis brilliant! How clever! What a bright wee mouse that Morris is!' But while they were clappin' Morris on the back and tellin' him how lucky they were to have him in the mice council, the oldest, wisest, most respected mouse arose. Now whenever he spoke, the others paid heed, and this is what he said. 'This plan that Morris has is very good. But let me ask ye one question. Who is goin' to hang the bell around the cat's neck?' The mice were struck silent. And as ye can well imagine, none o' them wanted the task."

Cambel giggled.

"The moral, Da, the moral!" cried Colin.

Brochan obliged him. "'Tis far easier to say a thing should be done than to do it."

Colin nudged her. "'Tis a good moral, aye?"

She nodded.

Cambel added, "Da says 'tisn't good enough to be a man o' words. Ye must be a man o' deeds."

"Speakin' o' deeds," Brochan said, "ye lads haven't milked the coos yet this eve."

"Come on, Colin," Cambel said, jumping up from the table. "Let's be men o' deeds."

"Will ye come with us, m'lady?" Colin said. "We'll show ye how we milk the coos."

It was on the tip of her tongue to tell him she already knew how to milk cows. Then she reconsidered.

There was one way she could find out if Brochan loved her. One thing that would prove beyond doubt that he wasn't after a marriage of convenience. It would take great skill and great courage on her part, like belling a cat. But she had to try, because...sometimes it was necessary to be a woman of deeds.

So she smiled and let the lads take her by the hand out of the hall. She pretended not to notice Brochan's irritation with her for leaving before he had a chance to speak with her alone.

After several minutes of letting the lads show her their milking skills, Cristy left them to their cows, making the excuse that she had to fetch her missing arisaid pin from the dovecot.

Instead, with a backward glance, she stole quietly across the starlit slope, toward the burn that separated the Macintosh and Moffat properties.

If she'd been aware that the lads had seen her leave and would follow her, she would never have gone. By the time she discovered them, she was past the burn, down the road, past the tavern, and deep into the fields of her uncle's holding.

By then it was too late.

For the last mile, she'd had the queer sensation she

was being watched. She'd quickly discarded the idea as nonsense. Nobody but her reiving cousins roamed the Moffat holding at this hour.

But the feeling didn't go away. When she heard distant footfalls behind her, she wheeled around, half expecting to see Archibald and the others.

Instead, Cambel and Colin were thrashing through the weeds, trying to catch up with her.

Her heart sank. What the devil were they doing? Why had they followed her?

Before she could hold up a hand to stop him, Colin yelled out, "M'lady, wait for us!"

Fearing discovery by her kin, she put a warning finger of silence to her lips and hurried to meet them.

She crouched before them, whispering, "What are ye lads doin'?"

"Where are ye goin', m'lady?" Cambel whispered back.

Colin's face fell. "Were ye leavin' us?"

Her throat thickened at his sad expression. "Nay, I was only..." How could she explain? "I'm just bein' a woman o' deeds."

"What deeds?" Cambel wanted to know.

She rubbed a hand across her lips. What was she going to do with the lads? She'd come too far to turn back now. And if Brochan discovered his sons had gone missing, another quarter hour would make little difference in their return anyway.

She was tempted to make them wait in the woods while she did what she'd come to do. She knew if they swore on their honor to stay where she put them, she could rely upon their word.

But if any of her clan found them in the forest, they'd turn the lads in to Douglas. And Douglas wouldn't hesitate to use the Macintosh lads the way Macintosh had used Cristy—as hostages.

"What deed, m'lady?" Colin repeated.

There was only one thing to do.

"A deed that requires a special talent, which is why I'm so glad ye came." She squeezed their shoulders. "I could use your help."

When Brochan walked inside the byre, he expected to see the lads dawdling over the milking as they shared their skills with Cristy. Showing off was one thing, but they'd been out there for over an hour. It was past their bedtime, and he needed to find a moment alone with Cristy to see if he could repair the damage he'd done.

What he did not expect to find were full, abandoned milk buckets.

He frowned. Where had the wayward lads gone?

His first thought was the comet. Maybe Cristy had taken them out to the field to get a better look at it.

But he scoured the hillside, to no avail.

Then he wondered if they'd gone to the dovecot. When he ducked inside, it was dark and empty.

Exiting, he narrowed his eyes at the herd of cattle. Could they be out there with the cows?

"Cambel!" he called out. "Colin!"

There was no reply.

A sickly fear prickled at the back of his neck.

Where was Cristy?

She'd been upset. Even at dinner, he could see she wasn't eating. He'd said that stupid thing about her uncle not wanting her back. He couldn't blame her for feeling hurt.

Was she hurt enough to seek retribution?

"Colin!" he shouted. "Cambel!"

He told himself she wouldn't do the lads any harm. They adored her, and she seemed to care for them.

But then he remembered what else he'd said. He'd told Cristy that no child of his would be raised in her uncle's household. He'd threatened to take her bairn away if she had one. And she'd been just as insistent that she wouldn't let him.

Was she upset enough to take *his* children?

A twinge of alarm twisted his heart. If she wished to wound him, she'd pierced him in his softest spot. The lads were everything to him.

He steeled his jaw. Normally, he was a peaceful man. But he'd once been a warrior. And when it came to his sons, he'd take on the entire Moffat clan for them.

Unwilling to waste another moment, he strode with determined haste to the tower to fetch his blade.

Once armed and ready, he stalked with purpose across his fields, past his cattle, and over the burn that divided the properties, his hand clenched around the hilt of his naked sword. Fear had no place in battle, so he pushed down the dread that threatened to unman him.

As he covered the miles between the properties, passing the tavern and leaving the road to trespass onto Moffat land, he thought only of his sons and the brute into whose hands they'd been delivered.

Indeed, so intent was he on mustering his courage that he didn't even see the lads until he was almost upon them. When he finally spied them cresting a distant brae, coming his way, he was so filled with relief that at first he was blind to everything except Colin and Cambel.

With renewed hope, he sheathed his sword and bounded toward them.

Then he saw Cristy. And the cows.

Slowing his step, he frowned. What the devil was she up to?

While he watched them, he saw Cristy guiding the lads, keeping a careful pace behind them as they herded one, two, three, four, five cows.

Chapter 11

Cristy spied the approaching figure before the lads did. How had Brochan arrived so fast? She'd hoped to have his sons home before he realized they were missing. God's eyes, he was probably furious. She only prayed he'd have enough sense not to bellow at her while they were still on Moffat land.

"Keep the coos movin', lads," she murmured. "Don't look now, but your Da is comin' this way. We can't let him scare the cattle."

Colin whimpered. "Och, nay."

"He'll be so vexed with us," Cambel said.

"He'll be vexed at *me*," Cristy assured them.

"But he'll be glad to have the coos back, aye?" Colin asked hopefully.

She wondered. Once Brochan had his five cows, he'd no longer have an excuse to keep her. So if he wanted her to stay—and she was almost certain he did—he'd have to give her a good reason. And it would have to be more convincing than needing a mother for his sons, help for his housekeeper, or a last name for her bastard.

The closer Brochan got, the more furious he looked. When he finally drew close enough to keep pace with them, his expression was tense, and his words were clipped. "Are these my coos?"

"Aye."

Cambel said, "M'lady is bringin' them back for ye, Da."

"I don't want them back," he ground out.

His words were meant for her, but the twins gasped in surprise.

"That was the agreement," she said. "Ye get your coos. I get my freedom."

"I won't take them back," he insisted.

She frowned. "Ye have to take them back."

"I refuse."

"Ye can't refuse."

"I do refuse."

The lads suddenly became far more interested in the argument taking place than guiding the cows. They halted, which made the cattle halt.

Cristy stopped, crossing her arms in challenge. "So ye'd rather keep me hostage than get your coos back?"

Brochan stopped, crossing his arms in defiance. "That's right."

"Why?"

He glowered at her.

"Ye've got your coos now and your sons," she said. "Why will ye not take them and let me go? Ye were happy enough before. Why not put things back the way they were?"

He averted his eyes and mumbled something under his breath.

"What?" she asked. "I didn't quite hear that."

His sons were staring at him, awaiting his reply. He scowled, squirming beneath their regard. Then he muttered something again.

She furrowed her brows. "I still didn't catch the words. Did ye, lads?"

The twins shook their heads.

"Perhaps ye could speak up a bit?" she suggested.

Her words might sound sincere, but he could hardly miss the mischief sparking in her eyes.

"Lucifer's ballocks," he said under his breath, shaking his head. Then he threw his arms wide and yelled at the top of his lungs. "Because I love ye, Cristy Moffat!"

She had no time to enjoy his heartfelt declaration. An instant after he shouted, chaos erupted. The cows, startled by the loud noise, scattered. In an effort to protect the lads, she scooped Cambel into her arms while Brochan swept up Colin.

They managed to keep the twins from harm until the cows had run off and they could put the lads down.

But in the next moment, she heard faraway cries of alarm. Moffat's watchmen had been alerted. They knew they were there.

"Run!" she hissed.

They wasted no time, bolting toward Macintosh land

as fast as they could. They tore across the grasslands, leaped over rocks, and charged through clumps of heather. When the lads began to fall behind on the road that led past the tavern, Brochan picked them up and carried one on each shoulder. By the time they reached the burn, Cristy could make out a half dozen torchlights in the distance, following them.

They forded the burn and didn't stop running until they were well across Brochan's own border, halfway back to the tower.

At last, too exhausted to continue, Cristy stopped, bending forward at the waist and bracing her hands on her knees. Her lungs burned, and she could hardly catch her breath. Brochan wheezed, his chest heaving as he set the lads back on their feet.

Suddenly the situation struck her as uproariously funny. She couldn't believe she'd gone to all the trouble to reive back his cows, only to have Brochan scatter them all with one outburst. She stifled a laugh.

Brochan must have seen the humor as well, for he looked at her with a sheepish snicker.

She began to giggle.

He chuckled in answer.

One laugh fueled the next. Soon they were overcome with laughter, collapsing onto the ground in uncontrollable hilarity.

The lads frowned down at them.

"What are ye laughin' for?" Colin asked. "We lost the coos again."

"Aye, what's so funny?" Cambel demanded.

Neither Brochan nor she were in any shape to reply. They were laughing too hard. But apparently their humor was catching, because soon the twins joined in until they were helpless with giggles.

When everyone finally sobered, breathless and weary, they made their way back to the tower house.

"Da," Cambel asked when they were almost to the motte, "did ye mean what ye said? Do ye love m'lady?"

Cristy's heart melted when Brochan looked at her and said, "Aye, I do."

"More than coos?" he asked.

He grinned. "Aye, Colin, more than coos."

Cambel asked, "Does she love ye back?"

"Ye'll have to ask *her* that."

Cambel raised his brows to her. "Well?"

"I do," Cristy replied with a smile, adding, "more than coos."

"Are ye goin' to stay with us then?" Cambel asked.

"Are ye goin' to be our Ma?" Colin added.

From the corner of her eye, Cristy saw Brochan tense. And she realized why he'd had such a difficult time confessing his love. He may have lost his wife five years ago. But he was a man of loyalty and chivalry. No doubt it was difficult to let go of his vows, even those that no longer had meaning.

So Cristy crouched down to answer Colin. "No one will e'er be able to replace your Ma, lads. But if your Da will have me, I'll do my best to love ye like a mother."

When she glanced up at Brochan, she could tell by his grateful gaze that her answer pleased him. And when the lads began to cheer and dance about, she knew she'd said the right thing.

Brochan was silent as they climbed the motte and entered the keep. But after handing the twins off to Mabel and hanging up his sword, he took Cristy by the hand.

"Will ye tuck the lads into bed?" he murmured to Mabel. "Miss Moffat and I would like to watch the comet alone tonight."

Cristy couldn't help but shiver with anticipation at his suggestion.

Mabel, who was hardly naïve, took the twins in hand and gave Cristy a wink. "Come along, lads," she said, "and I'll tell ye the story o' *The Ant and the Grasshopper.*"

As Brochan spread his gray woolen brat for Cristy on the crest of the motte, he felt like a changed man. Propped on his elbow beside her, gazing out at his woods, his fields, his slumbering herd of cattle, he no longer saw an overwhelming responsibility, but a shared vision. Now that he'd let Cristy into his heart, it seemed a weight had been lifted from his shoulders. He was no longer alone.

He threaded his fingers through hers as they looked up at the shimmering comet.

"Do ye think 'tis true?" she murmured.

"What?"

"That ye can change your stars?"

"I know 'tis true," he said.

She smiled. "'Twas the comet that brought us together, ye know."

"I know."

She leaned her head against his as she gazed up at the comet. "I think the star is starin' down on us now and smilin'."

He turned to kiss her brow. "Do ye think it might be willin' to close its eyes for a wee bit?"

Cristy grinned. "I think it would be more than willin'."

Brochan had never made love under the stars. But he was feeling transformed, and somehow it seemed the right thing to do.

He lifted Cristy's hand and kissed her knuckles. Her lips parted, and he leaned forward to capture them between his own.

His blood went from warm to fiery in an instant. A roaring rush of desire flowed through his ears. He felt the tug of need in his trews before the kiss ended.

But he didn't want to hurry. Their first tryst had been impulsive and frantic. He'd given little thought to anything but slaking his thirst.

He wanted this joining to be special. This time, he'd give her the patience and care she deserved.

Brushing the hair back from her face, he pressed a soft kiss to each eyelid.

She sighed in pleasure and placed a hand on his chest.

He kissed her sweet mouth again, letting his fingers drift along her temples, across her cheeks, and along her neck, leaving a trail of feather-light touches that made her quiver.

Slipping his fingers beneath the neck edge of her kirtle, he gently nudged it from her shoulder. Then, tipping her head aside, he placed a row of slow and deliberate kisses from the point of her shoulder up to her ear.

By the time he reached her ear, she was squirming in lusty torment. When he caught the delicate lobe between his teeth, she gasped. And when he let his tongue slip around the rim, she moaned with need.

He let out a worldly chuckle. She might grow impatient, but he still had a long way to go. They had all night, after all, and he intended to show the inexperienced lass every delicious enticement he knew.

Cristy didn't want to wait. She'd waited her whole life to belong. And now that she'd found the man with whom she could share her laughter, her tears, her fears and hopes, she didn't wish to waste another moment. She wanted to share her body with him. Now.

With desperate haste, before he could stop her, she unlaced her kirtle. She dragged it, along with her linen leine, down over her shoulders and past her hips, kicking the garments off her legs. While his jaw was still gaping, she lunged forward into his arms, rocking him onto his back.

The kiss she stole was full of passion and promise, fire and heart. It was the kiss she'd been saving all her life.

After his initial shock, Brochan answered her caresses, licking tenderly at her lips and weaving his fingers through the curtain of her hair.

The ache between her thighs was powerful and

compelling. And now that she knew the joy to come, she couldn't help but wish to hurry.

She fumbled at his trews, eager to free that amazing part of him that would grant her relief.

He caught her fingers and unlaced his trews himself. Then, taking control again, he clasped the back of her head. Wrapping his arm around her bare waist, he rolled with her until she lay on her back at the edge of the woolen brat.

From here, she could see the stars sparkling overhead like raindrops against the peat-dark sky. But when she shifted her gaze, she saw something even more beautiful. Brochan's eyes were glistening with love and desire.

Slowly, he removed his own garments, and she felt the twinge of yearning with every inch of skin he exposed. He belonged to her now—this magnificent man with the broad shoulders and wide chest, breathtaking arms and towering legs, a chivalrous spirit and a loving heart.

When he came to her, their joining was tender. This time there was no pain, only fulfillment. And when they rode together on passion's heavenly comet, a pure white light seemed to bless their union. Faster and faster they shot across the sky until the brilliant light shattered and scattered into a thousand bright stars.

Afterward, they lay together, side-by-side and hand-in-hand, gazing up at the night sky. They spoke of dreams and plans and wishes for the future. They mused over the gardens they would plant, the animals they would keep for the twins, and the Macintosh bairns they would make. And they marveled over the strange woman it seemed they'd both met at the tavern by chance, wondering whether it had been by chance at all.

As Cristy stared at the curious comet that had crossed her path and changed her fortune, she couldn't help but believe in the magic of the summer star.

The End

CHANK YOU FOR
READING MY BOOK!

Did you enjoy it? If so, I hope you'll post a review to let others know! There's no greater gift you can give an author than spreading your love of her books.

It's truly a pleasure and a privilege to be able to share my stories with you. Knowing that my words have made you laugh, sigh, or touched a secret place in your heart is what keeps the wind beneath my wings. I hope you enjoyed our brief journey together, and may ALL of your adventures have happy endings!

If you'd like to keep in touch, feel free to sign up for my monthly e-newsletter at www.glynnis.net, and you'll be the first to find out about my new releases, special discounts, prizes, promotions, and more!

If you want to keep up with my daily escapades:
Friend me at facebook.com/GlynnisCampbell
Like my Page at bit.ly/GlynnisCampbellFBPage
Follow me at twitter.com/GlynnisCampbell
And if you're a super fan, join
facebook.com/GCReadersClan

ÐANGER'S KISS

Medieval Outlaws Book 1

he spotted Desirée at once, by the light of a moonbeam filtering through the shutters. She was asleep, luxuriously sprawled across the coverlet like a cat with a belly full of cream, commandeering his pallet as if her spindly frame required every inch of it.

"Oh, nay, you don't," he murmured. He might feel sorry for the orphaned lass, but he wasn't about to let her usurp his bed. "Desirée," he called.

She didn't move.

"Desirée."

Still no reply.

He drew closer, not close enough that she could swing out with a stray fist and clip him on the jaw, but close enough to be heard.

"Desirée."

She still didn't stir, but Azrael, tucked behind one of her knees, lifted his head.

Nicholas frowned. There was something tied around the cat's neck. Something distinctly feminine.

"God's eyes! What have you done to my cat?"

That woke her. She rose on her elbows, her eyes glazed, her mouth making sleepy smacks. "What?"

"What did you do to Azrael?"

She glanced down at the cat, as if trying to recall. Then her lips curved up in a smile that was pure mischief. "He thinks it's pretty," she said, crooning, "doesn't he, Snowflake?"

Nicholas seized Azrael, who yowled once in complaint, and immediately untied the silly bow, dropping it atop the coverlet.

Desirée shrugged off his actions and snuggled back down under the blankets. "Did you get my list?" she murmured.

He gave Azrael a consoling pat and set him down again on the pallet. "Your list? You mean that nonsense about lavender and beeswax candles? Do you know how much saffron costs?"

"Come, Nicky, you can't expect me to keep your house properly if I don't have the required supplies."

"I seem to have done fine before without them. And stop calling me Nicky."

"What would you prefer? Your Majesty?"

Nicholas exhaled on a growl, trying to recall why he'd felt sorry for the pesky imp. "I've bought another pallet. I've placed it beside the fire."

"Mm, good," she purred. "I'd hate to think of you getting cold in the night."

He blinked. The audacity of the naughty wench was amazing. Unable to think of a fitting verbal response, he decided to let his actions speak for him. He threw back the covers and, ignoring her indignant shrieks, scooped her up into his arms.

"Unhand me, sirrah!"

"You're not sleeping in my bed." He started toward the door.

"But I was there first!"

"'Tis *my* bed."

"You weren't using it." She actually wedged her limbs in the doorway, trying to prevent his exit.

"Well, I'm going to use it now."

"'Tisn't fair!"

He didn't feel like arguing the absurdity of a tiny lass expropriating his huge bed while he lay cramped on a small pallet by the fire.

"The only way you're sleeping in that bed," he whispered wickedly, "is if you're sharing it with me."

ABOUT THE AUTHOR

I'm a *USA Today* bestselling author of swashbuckling action-adventure historical romances, mostly set in Scotland, with over a dozen award-winning books published in six languages.

But before my role as a medieval matchmaker, I sang in *The Pinups,* an all-girl band on CBS Records, and provided voices for the MTV animated series *The Maxx,* Blizzard's *Diablo* and *Starcraft* video games, and *Star Wars* audiobooks.

I'm the wife of a rock star (if you want to know which one, contact me) and the mother of two young adults. I do my best writing on cruise ships, in Scottish castles, on my husband's tour bus, and at home in my sunny southern California garden.

I love transporting readers to a place where the bold heroes have endearing flaws, the women are stronger than they look, the land is lush and untamed, and chivalry is alive and well!

I'm always delighted to hear from my readers, so please feel free to email me at glynnis@glynnis.net. And if you're a super-fan who would like to join my inner circle, sign up at http://www.facebook.com/GCReadersClan, where you'll get glimpses behind the scenes, sneak peeks of works-in-progress, and extra special surprises!

www.ingramcontent.com/pod-product-compliance
Lightning Source LLC
Chambersburg PA
CBHW020522120726
47904CB00003B/939